INFESTATION

Inspired by True Events

CHERYL KAYE TARDIF

INFESTATION

www.cherylktardif.com

FIRST EDITION Trade Paperback

September 1, 2016

Published by Imajin Qwickies®, an imprint of Imajin Books®

www.ImajinQwickies.com

ISBN: 978-1-77223-276-9

Cover designed by Ryan Doan: www.ryandoan.com

Prologue
"Secrets"

Every house has its secrets, some more perverse and horrific than others.

Rooms bear witness to the lives of those within, while floors hold traces of footprints from all who have trampled there. Minuscule, airborne particles of skin, hair and blood from countless occupants float throughout, captured only for a fleeting moment by a ray of sunlight. The walls and floors of a house imperceptibly expand and contract with every inhalation, as though alive and breathing.

But where there is life, there is also death. All living things return to the earth...eventually. Such is the circle of life and death, forever intertwined in the intimate dance of destiny.

If a house could tell stories…

Chapter 1
"Mama, I'm Coming Home"

Leaning against the deck rail of her new home, forty-two-year-old Cathy Tremblay sipped a glass of Okanagan wine and watched cotton-ball clouds float over the valley, while pale rays from a slow-setting summer sun kissed the mountain ridges with soft pink and gold tones.

"I'm home," she murmured.

Ecstatic to be back in her home province of British Columbia after spending the past twenty-two years in Alberta, she could now return to her former self-imposed label of 'BC suspense author,' and her cable-installer husband, Mike, wouldn't have to work in such harsh outdoor conditions. Their life seemed perfect here—slower paced, peaceful and inspiring.

"I can't believe we get to look at this view every day now," she said. "The only way this could be any better is if we had a lake view."

"You said you wanted a *water* view, and you got it." Mike, a year younger than Cathy, pointed to the above-ground pool covered with a blue tarp.

She gave him a wry smile. "Not quite what I meant, but I'll take it."

Located in the rolling mountains of West Kelowna, BC, the rancher-style home with walkout basement was fifteen years old and sat on a half-acre of mature mountainside. The front yard showcased a variety of conifers, including a pristine blue spruce. Centered in the lawn stood a golden maple, a wooden birdhouse with faded blue paint haphazardly wedged between the branches. A Japanese red maple caressed the left side of the house. Stone steps led down the right side to the landscaped backyard, which featured an assortment of rose bushes and other shrubs, two maples and a row of sentinel-like cedars that protected the occupants from falling over the steep incline of the property.

The house had three bedrooms on the main floor level, and an open-concept kitchen, dining, and living room with a fireplace. The main floor bathroom featured a shower/tub combination, while the en-suite bathroom off the master bedroom had a glass shower separate from the over-sized soaker tub under the large picture window. When bathing, Cathy liked to keep the electric blind up so she could watch the birds scavenging for berries from the mountain ash that grew outside the window.

A large part of the basement had been converted by past homeowners into a two-bedroom, self-contained suite with an office nook looking out over the backyard. Mike's "Man Cave" and a massive storage area completed the lower level. The suite was ideal for Margot, Cathy's sixty-four-year-old mother, who'd been living alone since her divorce.

Her mother loathed living in Port Coquitlam—or any big city, for that matter. She'd always talked of retiring in the Okanagan one day. So they'd invited her to live with them. At the moment, Margot was visiting Cathy's brother, Darryl, and his family in Halifax and wouldn't be home for two weeks.

"Mom really loves it here," she said to Mike. "Thanks for agreeing to let her move in with us."

"I love your mom, too." Mike smirked. "She's easy to live with."

"Are you insinuating I'm *not*?"

"I would never do such a thing," he teased. "I can't believe you think that."

"I can't believe the bank let this house go for such a low price. Makes me wonder what's wrong with it."

"Nothing's wrong with the house, Cathy. I spoke with Les, next door, and he said that the previous owners up and left in the middle of the night."

"That's awfully suspicious, isn't it? What were they into—drugs?"

"The bank had the house inspected and the air tested. No grow-op or meth lab on the premises. No one knows why they left. But just be glad they did, or we wouldn't be living here." He wrapped his arms around her. "You know, for our first pre-owned home, we did pretty well."

"I guess."

Cathy had always said she'd never own an existing home owned by others. To her, it was like taking on someone else's headaches and problems. She'd heard too many horror stories about people buying money pits. Last thing they needed was their home falling apart all around them, which is why she loved building from scratch. Why borrow trouble?

Nevertheless, she'd caved for Mike. Thankfully, the house inspector hadn't found anything wrong with the house, inside or out.

She peered over his shoulder at the windows that lined the back of the house. "I have to admit, I really like this place. And isn't it ironic that all the rooms, including the guest room and my home office, are painted in colors matching our décor? I even got the seafoam-colored bedroom I've wanted."

"Good. Because I sure don't plan on spending the weekends painting."

"I still miss my dream kitchen, though." She smirked. "I can't wait to renovate this one."

They had built their first two homes in Edmonton, with Cathy designing the ultimate chef's kitchen in the last one. Mike's pride and joy had been the three-car garage with the heated floor. He was down to a small two-car garage now, with room beside the driveway for an RV or boat. Or jet skis.

"The kitchen doesn't need renovating," Mike said. "Sure, the cupboards are ugly and the counter is cheap laminate, but they're in decent shape."

Cathy gaped at him. "Are you kidding me? Someone sanded the cupboards then painted over cheap melamine. I'm getting my kitchen eventually. And you always say, 'Happy wife; happy life.' You want me to be happy, right?"

He chuckled. "Remind me to shut my mouth next time."

She kissed him. "I'm going inside."

"You heading to bed?"

She nodded. "Yeah, I'm beat."

"I love you."

"Love you, too." She paused in the doorway. "Oh, before you leave on your trip tomorrow, please don't forget to throw all those 'For Sale' signs in the recycle bin. We don't want to attract pests."

"I won't."

* * *

Mike recalled his wife's request a few hours later, after spending the evening star gazing and finishing off the bottle of wine. With a sigh, he went inside, pulled on a pair of sneakers and shuffled off to the garage.

The signs were stacked against the wall by a chest freezer. He lifted the heavy wood slabs, and something caught his eye. "Ah, shit."

Fresh scratches on the posts indicated that something had been feasting. Mice, maybe. Although he'd heard there were rats in the Okanagan, he hadn't divulged this morsel of knowledge to his wife. Rodents in the garage would not go over well with Cathy. She had an intense dislike of insects, spiders and rodents—entomophobic, arachnophic and musophobic—especially if they were anywhere near her.

Mike pushed the electronic door button and the garage door groaned as it rose. Gathering the signs into his arms, he strode outside and tossed everything into the bin around the corner. It took him three trips to clear out the rotted wood.

Back in the garage, he moved the boxes closer to his work truck and inspected the finished walls and concrete floor. No sign of shit anywhere, and nothing appeared to be damaged. One piece of loose drywall was the only thing that stood out.

He yanked on the panel of drywall and it came away in chunks, revealing shredded insulation inside. He'd have to buy a sheet of drywall when he returned from his trip.

Mike was about to turn away when the insulation moved. "What the hell?"

He poked the pink fiber, and something moved again. With vigilant movements, he used the claw of a hammer to peel back the insulation. Beneath the insulation, five newborn rodents ravenously suckled at their mother's swollen teats. She barely blinked at the intrusion.

Mice?

He leaned in to get a closer look. *Shit!* The mother's tail was bushy, not bare, and she looked a bit like a squirrel. These weren't mice.

Pack rats!

He'd heard about them from Les, who'd had one in his garage next door. Pack rats had bushy tails and were often mistaken for squirrels. Mike recalled the day Cathy said she'd spotted a gray squirrel sitting on the fence in the backyard. Perhaps it hadn't been a squirrel after all. He couldn't tell Cathy that.

He took a fortifying breath. "Sorry, but you can't stay here."

Freeing the rats would only be asking for their future return. If he gave them to a pet store, they'd probably be sold as snake food. That left only one option.

Killing innocent animals wasn't Mike's thing.

But sometimes it had to be done.

* * *

Concealed by shadows, it watched the human, knowing that if it moved, a violent death would follow. So it remained still, its loathing gaze fixated on the human who'd invaded its territory and murdered its family.

It would get its revenge.

Chapter 2
"Trouble"

By 3:30 Monday afternoon, Cathy had completed all editing and other busy work, including writing down plot notes for a thriller about a deadly epidemic spreading across the valley. The new novel was going to be her "big one." She knew it deep in her aching bones.

"Now what to do?"

Talking to herself wasn't anything new. She engaged in the activity habitually, particularly when she was writing or concentrating on numbers and math. It helped with the long, lonely days and nights when Mike was on the road with work.

Like today.

Mike had left before dawn. He'd be out of town for a week, which meant Cathy could devote all her time to writing, and she could eat when she wanted to—or not. Today, she'd already traded breakfast and lunch for two coffees.

What next? "Take a break."

She decided to indulge in one of her few guilty pleasures and watch *Days of Our Lives*, the daytime soap she'd watched ever since she was a teen. She'd grown up with the cast, particularly Kayla and Patch, Bo and Hope. But the death toll in Salem was rising. They'd killed off half the cast in the past year, or so it seemed. EJ, Serena, Paige, Will, Bo—all gone. Even the devilish Stefano DiMera appeared to be dead, three shots to the chest by Hope Brady.

When the show was over, Cathy tossed a load of laundry into the washer and folded the clean-but-wrinkled load that had been in the basket for over a week. Then she threw ingredients into the bread maker and checked her sales ranks on Amazon. The latter was another guilty pleasure.

The cuckoo clock she'd inherited from her German grandmother gonged five times. *Time to get up and move around.*

"Ah," she moaned.

Her hips ached with every step. There was a downside to sitting all day, besides the unwanted pounds she'd gained over the years. She suffered from a painful genetic disorder called Hypermobility Syndrome, one of the "invisible" conditions. Chronic pain flowed through her body like blood through veins, and knifelike heat seared through her joints when she stretched.

Dr. Sawyer told her the connective tissue in her body was breaking down like old elastic bands. "And what happens to old elastics when you overstretch them?" he'd asked.

She'd cringed. "They break."

No impact exercises for her. The only workouts recommended were walking, swimming and careful stretching. How the hell was she supposed to lose weight when her body wouldn't cooperate?

A creaking sound reverberated behind her.

Cathy spun on one heel, lost her balance and executed a less than graceful shuffle to right herself. Spatial recognition and vertigo were also common with HMS sufferers. Escalators at the mall and dim stairwells were the worst. Some days she had trouble walking downstairs. She'd even managed to perfect tripping *up*stairs.

Creeeeak...

The sound seemed to be coming from inside the wall near the kitchen island.

"Must be the pipes," she said, unconvinced.

She imagined Mike saying, "New houses always make strange noises. You'll just have to get used to them."

He was right, of course.

* * *

Cathy shuffled into the bedroom at 2:30 in the morning, praying she'd be able to sleep. New plot ideas always sent her mind into a tailspin. She made her way to the en-suite bathroom, using the nightlight on the wall at the far end to guide her. As she passed blindly through the doorframe, a strand of hair tickled her forehead.

In the bathroom, she turned on a soft light and completed her nightly routine. After she brushed her teeth, she reached for her evening medications. A little Nexium for acid reflux, some useless Tramadol for HMS pain and one amitriptyline tablet to help her deal with an overstimulated mind—or "to quiet the voices in her head," as she liked to tell Mike.

She felt the same faint tickle on her face as she passed under the doorway. Ignoring the strange sensation, she slid between the sheets. Mike's body always emitted heat at night, but tonight she felt his absence in the coolness of the sheets.

She reached for the sleep apnea mask that hung from the bedpost. It was amazing how much better she slept since getting the CPAP machine. Before the sleep apnea diagnosis, she'd wake up every morning with a sore throat from snoring. And she'd wake up in the middle of the night to pee.

Not now, though.

Positioning the nose piece in her nostrils, she tapped the button of the machine and inhaled deeply. Something tickled the back of her throat—dust, most likely—and she ripped the mask from her nose and coughed until she gagged. She repositioned the nose piece and stretched out diagonally on the king-sized bed, her favorite position when Mike was gone.

Then she slept.

* * *

Cathy spent Tuesday working on the epidemic thriller, and by midday she'd written over six thousand words. Satisfied, she shut down her laptop and prepared a meal of fried chicken livers with bacon and onions, something she only ate when Mike was away.

As a reward for an awesome writing day, she settled in front of the television and binge-watched five episodes of *Supernatural*. By the time she'd finished the fifth one, she was jittery and paranoid. She could almost hear Mike's voice in her head saying, "It's just a TV show. It's not real. Nothing to worry about."

What the hell was she thinking? Here she was, alone in an empty house, her mother and husband miles away, and she was watching horror shows, something she usually only did during daylight hours.

She shivered and glanced outside at the darkening sky.

Okay, enough. Think of something else.

To clear her troubled mind from visions of Sam and Dean hunting lethal paranormal creatures, she decided to give herself a facial while watching an episode of *Last Man Standing*. Tim Allen always made her laugh.

In the en-suite bathroom, she arranged the various skincare products on the counter. Removing her eyeglasses, she slid a hairband over her head and arranged it so it held back the red and blonde streaks that barely touched her shoulders.

Her forehead itched. So did the back of her neck. The more she scratched, the more she itched.

"No more *Supernatural* for you at night," she warned her reflection.

She scrubbed her face and slathered on the clay mask. With a chuckle at her slowly-hardening pale face, she returned to the living room. Tim Allen and his TV family were up to their antics. Each time Cathy laughed, she felt the clay give way. She was literally cracking up—or at least her face was.

When the sitcom was over, she strode back to the bathroom to remove the mask. The lightest whisper of air made her forehead tingle, and she brushed her face with the back of one hand. Why did her skin always feel so damned itchy? The air in the Okanagan was moister than Edmonton, where she'd experienced dry skin regularly.

Even her feet were smoother here. Yet every time she stepped into the bathroom, a prickly feeling crept over her.

Needing more light to wash all the clay off her face, she flicked on the bright light over the bathtub. She reached for the washcloth and looked into the mirror. "What the—?"

The light above the bathtub revealed several fine threads dangling from the ceiling. Cobwebs? Hair? Whatever it was, it could only be seen in brighter light.

Setting down the cloth, she turned around in a slow circle.

"Oh my God..."

Hundreds of threads hung from the ceiling. And some were moving.

Spiders!

Cathy's hand flew to her mouth, muffling a yelp.

God, how she hated spiders.

* * *

At eighteen, Cathy had moved to Vancouver to take a cosmetology course. She'd rented a basement apartment owned by an elderly man, who later turned out to be a pervert who liked to spy on her when she showered.

One night, she'd found three black spiders with bulbous bodies hovering above her bed. At the time, she had no idea the red splotch on their backs meant they were black widows. She only knew they had to disappear—permanently.

So she'd grabbed a broom and attempted to kill them, except one escaped.

That night Cathy slept on the sofa.

The following day, she searched the bedroom, but the spider was nowhere to be seen. She pulled the bed away from the wall, vacuumed every inch of the threadbare carpet and washed all the bedding. That night she climbed into bed and fell into a restless sleep.

In the morning, she discovered a white patch on her chest. Her skin had been bleached out somehow. Every freckle was gone from that peculiar patch, and in the center was a tiny red dot. The black widow had left its mark.

Cathy never had a single decent night's sleep in that apartment. She was plagued by nightmares about spiders swarming her body while she slept.

She hadn't had one of those dreams in over twenty years.

* * *

Now Cathy stood in the center of the bathroom, afraid to breathe or move.

A minuscule spider rappelled down its thread a few inches from her head, and she backed away, recalling the feeling of something touching her bare shoulders the night before. Now she knew what it was.

Ugh!

Her skin crawled, and she resisted the urge to scratch. She wanted nothing more than to leave the bathroom, close the door and never enter it again, but that wouldn't solve the problem. And who knows where the spiders would travel to next. She had to get rid of them.

Her head ducked low, she retrieved the toilet brush from its stand. Armed with the weapon, she slowly swiped at the threads then held the brush under hot water. She'd boil those suckers alive.

She inched her way around the room, clearing the ceiling as she went.

"It's just hair," she kept telling herself.

In one corner she discovered a quarter-sized patch of what looked like lint. She poked at it with the end of the brush, and the patch exploded into dozens of tiny spiders.

Shit!

She'd disturbed a nest.

"No, no, no!"

Reaching under the sink, she grabbed a bottle of glass cleaner and sprayed anything that moved. With a wad of toilet paper stuck to the end of the brush, she wiped up the mess and tossed it into the toilet. She spent the next half hour swiping, spraying and flushing. When every trace of spiders, nests and threads were gone, she went over the entire bathroom with disinfectant spray.

She picked up her toothbrush. *What if spiders have been crawling all over it at night while I slept?* She rinsed it under scorching hot water and rubbed the bristles with her thumb.

It wasn't until she'd finished cleaning that she realized she hadn't washed her face. The facial mask had hardened, but her movements had created tiny fissures and cracks in the clay.

After a thorough cleanse, she brushed her teeth with the newly-sanitized toothbrush, closed the bathroom door, climbed into bed and called Mike.

"You should have seen them," she said, describing the spider adventure in the bathroom. "They were rappelling like Tom Cruise in a *Mission Impossible* movie. Except *their* acting was far better. Those spiders scared the shit out of me."

"But you handled it, right?"

"Yeah, but it was awful. I've scratched my skin raw, and I can't go in our bathroom. I'm afraid of what I'll find."

She heard him blow out an impatient huff. "Cathy, they're gone. You already scrubbed the bathroom. I doubt there are any spiders left."

"Why does this have to happen when I'm here alone?"

"I doubt Margot would've been much help."

"I meant you. And you'd be surprised. My mother doesn't get as freaked out as I do about bugs."

A low chuckle sounded from the other end of the line. "*Nobody* gets as freaked out as you do."

"You should've seen them. It was an infestation—hundreds of them crawling all over the ceiling. I'm sure I had them in my hair and on my face."

"Don't think about it. When I come back, I'll clean the bathroom ceiling again. Okay?"

"Okay. I love you, Mike."

"Love you, too. Bye for now."

Cathy watched another half-hour sitcom on the bedroom TV, hoping to purge from her mind the image of hundreds of miniscule spiders swarming the bathroom ceiling. It didn't work. Afterward, her gaze swept over the room, wondering where else spiders could be hiding, her imagination filling in the blanks. *Are they hanging from the ceiling over my bed? Or in the closet?*

She knew she was running on paranoia, but that didn't make her feel better.

The television distraction almost worked—until she turned off the TV and reached for her apnea mask.

She stared at the nosepiece. *What if spiders climbed inside?*

For the first night in over two years, she hung the apnea mask back on the post. In the morning she would soak the mask and hose in hot water. That would ensure the hose was clean and free from any foreign bodies. Including spiders.

That night Cathy fell into an agitated sleep, haunted by visions of hungry black widows and tiny spiders rappelling from every ceiling in the house. In her nightmare, they were coming for her...and there was no escape.

Chapter 3
"2 Heads"

On Wednesday afternoon, her third day of solitude, Cathy heard the doorbell ring. "Better not be Mormons," she muttered.

A week after moving in, she'd taped a sign on the front door that read, 'No newspapers, no flyers & no religious solicitation. Thank you!' But that didn't stop them from trying, especially the U-Tel guys. They were notorious for ignoring homeowners' signs.

As she approached the frosted glass door, she recognized the hunched silhouette on the other side. She opened the door. "Dad!"

Sixty-five-year-old Lars Kilborn was clean shaven, bald and had a slight beer belly. A former military spy—or "Double-Oh-Zero," as Cathy loved to call him—he now performed freelance computer work for her, formatted her novels and proofread them. He was a computer genius in her eyes. Coding, programming, spreadsheets—it all came naturally to him.

But not Cathy. If there was one thing she was no good at, it was numbers. She always told people, "I do words, not numbers." Plus she was dyslexic, something not everyone knew. Being in the public eye, even a writer had to keep some semblance of privacy.

"What are you doing here?" she asked her father.

"I wanted to show you something. I have a spreadsheet that shows every sale, every freebie, etcetera, for every title you've published."

"Are you staying the weekend? Mike's away, and I could use the company."

"Sure. I can do that."

Though her father lived in Penticton, about a forty-five minute drive away, she preferred that he not drive at night, so he kept extra clothes in the guest room. At least he was quiet. He typically passed out on the couch after an hour or so of computer conversation or a meal. Sometimes he'd fall asleep mid-sentence, his mouth open.

Tonight was no different.

Cathy discovered her father passed out on the recliner after Chinese takeout from Golden Chopsticks in West Kelowna. They made the best spicy ginger beef, Cathy's favorite.

"You're so predictable, Dad," she murmured.

While he slept, she continued to check emails on her laptop. When her father snored, at least he didn't sound like a freight train passing through the room, like Mike did.

By midnight she decided to wake him up and send him on his way to the guest room. "It's bedtime, Dad."

Bleary eyes blinked at her. "You going to bed?"

"Yeah," she lied. She began turning off the lights. "See you in the morning."

Once her father was settled for the evening, she snuck back into the living room and resumed her position on the recliner.

Some stories couldn't wait to be written. The one she had on her mind kept percolating, spawning more twists and enough red herrings to throw off even the most discerning reader.

Yeah, this was going to be the *big* one. She could feel it in her bones.

* * *

Cathy spent Thursday sightseeing with her father. They checked out a few wineries and sampled some Okanagan wine before heading for a late lunch at Rose's on Kelowna's waterfront. After devouring a mile-high plate of nachos and two iced teas out on the patio, they relaxed and watched various water vessels leave and return to the marina.

A wasp landed on her plate, wading into a blob of salsa before flying away.

I must be a bug magnet.

She surveyed the patio area and discovered she wasn't the only customer being hassled by the pests. Breathing a sigh of relief, she returned to her meal, until she caught sight of the waitress whacking wasps with a fly swatter. The woman's actions reminded Cathy of the spiders, and she told father about her late-night discovery.

"Of course this *has* to happen when Mike's out of town," she muttered. "The infestation couldn't have happened when he was here."

"Infestation?" Her father laughed. "I'm sure it wasn't that bad."

She sighed. "Why does everyone think I don't know the meaning of *infestation*? I can handle a few bugs or spiders. But hundreds of them hatching over my head? That's not my idea of a *'few.'*"

"You killed them all, right?"

"Yes, Dad. For now anyway." *Maybe they'll come back. Zombie spiders?*

When they returned home, her father disappeared downstairs with his laptop. He was such a workaholic. Some days Cathy wished he'd slow down. Then again, he did so much for her that she didn't know what she'd ever do without him.

She considered herself to be very fortunate. Both parents had supported her writing career, even though there'd been no guarantee of success. Her mother had invested financially in Cathy's first published book. In return, Margot earned royalties on that book and all of its subsidiary products.

Now Cathy was a *New York Times* and *USA Today* bestselling author. For the first time since they'd met, her income was higher than Mike's, and he sure didn't complain. He called her his "retirement plan."

* * *

While preparing supper that evening, Cathy opened the cupboard next to the fridge. A handful of tiny brown pellets rested on the bottom shelf. For a second she thought they were grains of rice. Then it hit her. "Ugh, this is gross."

"What's wrong?" her father asked from the living room.

"I found mouse turds in the cupboard." She opened another cabinet door. "More turds in this one. And pee stains, too. Damn it."

"Have you seen any mice?"

"No, thank God."

She recalled the day Mike had sworn he'd heard scratching inside the en-suite bathroom walls. She'd been positive the scratching sounds were from the branches of the mountain ash outside the window.

She shuddered. *What if there* are *mice inside the walls?*

The remainder of the evening was spent emptying cupboards and sanitizing every inch of the ones that showed evidence of rodents. She loaded up the dishwasher twice with the dishes from three cabinets. While cleaning, she discovered that a previous owner had added a gas line for a gas stove, and he'd drilled holes in the walls and cabinets. None of the holes had been sealed. She'd bet a million bucks this was how the wretched mouse was getting in.

Releasing a tired sigh, she flopped into the recliner across from her father. "Again I ask, why doesn't this happen when Mike's here?" She squirmed at the thought of a mouse running loose through the kitchen cabinets.

"We'll pick up some traps tomorrow."

"Sounds good, Dad."

That evening Cathy and her father watched an action flick and ate popcorn.

Every so often she'd look over at the kitchen, half-expecting a mouse to lunge out of a cupboard.

But nothing moved.

Chapter 4
"Fly Away"

After a trip to Home Depot Friday morning, Cathy was armed with two mouse traps, the spin kind that were supposed to be a more "humane" way to kill mice. She removed the traps from the packaging and loaded the bait area with peanut butter. Two of the three cupboards seemed to be the mouse's favorite—based on the amount of mouse turds she'd found—so she placed the traps there.

She went about her day, forgetting all about mice and turds.

It wasn't until she reached for the blender in the bottom cupboard that she remembered the trap. Without touching it, she could see it hadn't been activated.

No dead mouse yet.

She inspected the second trap in the other cupboard. It was empty, too.

"I, uh, checked downstairs," her father said as he shuffled into the kitchen, "and I found mouse turds on your mom's bed."

"Ew. I'll change her bedding right away."

"I bet Margot's going to be glad she was on holiday."

Cathy nodded. "We'd better be rid of this mouse before Mom returns. Hey, do you mind taking the garbage out and putting it in the bin?"

Her father grabbed the garbage bag from under the sink and disappeared into the garage. When he returned a few seconds later, his expression was a mix of "Uh-oh!" and "You're not going to like what I have to say."

"What now?" she said, groaning.

"Well…you have a little fly problem."

"Flies now?"

She wasn't afraid of flies. They were a nuisance more than anything else.

With a curse, Cathy strode into the garage, where she discovered the downside to being a courteous neighbor and not leaving the trash bin outside to attract bears. A dozen or so flies hovered above the bin.

"Great."

She pushed the garage door opener. Maybe the flies would take off outside. As she reached the trash bin, the flies dispersed. They flew around the garage then resumed their vigil over the bin. Holding her breath, she steered the bin onto the driveway and pushed open the lid.

A thick gray fog of flies rose into the air. Thousands of them.

With a small shriek, Cathy ran back inside the garage. Dozens of flies followed her, and she batted them away from her face. She pressed the garage door button then returned to the safety of her house.

"I don't get it," she said to her father. "Why so many flies? There are only two small bags in the trash bin."

"Did you throw out any raw meat or meat packaging?"

She shrugged. "Maybe. But nothing different from any other week."

"Must be something in there that's drawing them in."

"Whatever is attracting them, that bin can stay outside." *So much for being a responsible neighbor.*

The remainder of Friday afternoon was spent laundering her mother's bedding and vacuuming the downstairs suite. Other than a few mouse turds on the bedspread, Cathy didn't find any signs of mice in the basement level. She did note, however, that her mother's bedroom was situated directly beneath the upstairs kitchen. The mouse must have chewed a tunnel from upstairs to down inside the walls.

Next, she combed through her upstairs office, praying no rodent had crossed into her lair. She inspected the shelves and desk. No trace of a mouse.

By evening, she was exhausted—not only from the chores but also from being on such high alert. She ordered pizza. No way was she cooking in that kitchen until they'd caught the mouse. Now that two traps were in place, it shouldn't take long. She tried not to think of rodents while she watched TV with her father. Once he fell asleep, she worked on the thriller for a couple of hours.

At 9:30, she took a break and went into the kitchen for a drink.

Scratch, scratch.

A shiver of dread slithered up her spine.

Scratch...

She reached out a hand. With slow movements, she opened the cupboard. Leaning low, she peered into the shadows and stopped breathing. Beside the black plastic trap in the back of the cabinet sat a gray mouse. It wriggled its nose, sniffing at her, yet it didn't move away. It made no attempt to step inside the trap, either.

Eat the bait!

Cathy glared at the mouse. It stared back, unperturbed by her presence.

"Okay, Mickey, this Mexican standoff has got to end. Climb in the trap."

Mickey remained still.

She slammed the cupboard door, partly out of frustration and partly because she hoped the mouse would be so scared he'd leave her house entirely.

"What time is it?" her father asked.

"The mousing hour."

"What?"

"It's 9:30, Dad. By the way, I just saw the mouse in the cupboard."

"Don't wait around in the kitchen," he advised. "Or you'll never catch him."

"All I'm waiting for now is the sound of the trap snapping shut."

The phone rang. It was Mike.

"I can't talk long," he said. "How's the spider problem?"

"I killed them all, I think." She sighed. "We now have a mouse in the house."

Mike chuckled. "Sounds like a Dr. Seuss book."

"Yeah—no. It's not that fun. Or funny."

"Did you buy some traps?"

"Of course. I put two in the cupboards where I found mouse turds and pee stains. I opened one tonight, and the little bastard was sitting right beside the trap, staring at me."

"Give it a day, and I bet you'll have him in that trap."

She didn't want to think about the mouse's lifeless body inside the hunk of plastic, but it was better than seeing its nearly decapitated head caught in a traditional trap.

"Besides that infuriating mouse, I also had to deal with an infestation of flies in the garage."

"There you go again. You've really got to relax, Cathy. There are bugs and mice in BC. We had them in Edmonton, too." His voice had that irritated edge to it.

"Not like this," she argued. "The trash bin was full of flies, and now so is your garage. I'm keeping the bin outside now, regardless of bears. And once you have a few days off, you need to build a shed for all three bins."

"Great. Another project."

"I miss you, Mike."

"You mean you miss my awesome spider smooshing, mouse trapping, fly swatting expertise."

She laughed. "That, too."

"I'll be home in a few days."

"Safe travels."

* * *

Before bed, Cathy decided to check on the fly situation. She strolled out into the jet-black night, and the motion sensor light came on as she rounded the corner. The bin appeared to be undisturbed, and the lid was still open.

She moved closer. *No sign of flies. Do they sleep at night?*

Faint movements on the ground caught her attention.

Maggots.

Dozens of fly larvae, resembling fat grains of rice, wriggled their plump, pale bodies around the base of the bin. In some areas they were four or five deep. Two stray maggots slithered down the side of the bin.

Her stomach churned as she watched the disgusting bugs writhe and squirm. She muffled a gag and made a beeline for the garage. Once inside, she hit the button to close the garage door.

"This is ridiculous," she muttered. "First spiders. Then a mouse, flies and maggots. What's next?"

She shouldn't have asked.

Chapter 5
"Radioactive"

On Saturday, day six without Mike, Cathy and her father drove out to Mission Hill Family Estate for lunch. Once through the contemporary arched entrance, they strolled around the massive property, taking in the expansive vineyards that overlooked Okanagan Lake. The architecture and grounds at Mission Hill were spectacular, making it a popular attraction for tourists and wine lovers.

For a few hours Cathy forgot all about the unwanted house pests that threatened to take over her home. Inhaling deeply, she breathed the fresh mountain air and said a prayer of gratitude to the universe for bringing her home.

"I can't get enough of this view," she said to her father. "I feel so comfortable here, like I've always lived in the Okanagan Valley."

"It *is* beautiful."

On the way back, Cathy stopped for steaks at G & H Shop & Save, her favorite grocery store off Boucherie Road. She selected two large baking potatoes, a container of sour cream, an apple pie and a brick of cheddar. Rather than vanilla ice cream, her father preferred a slice of cheese on warm apple pie.

They barbecued the steaks out on the deck and watched the sun set as they ate.

"You can hear the traffic on the highway," her father said.

"Yeah, but it's white noise. Doesn't bother me at all. I find it comforting."

Her father set his plate on the patio table. "I'm stuffed."

She snickered beneath her breath. "So you won't want any apple pie then."

"Well, I'm never too full for pie."

"How did I know you were gonna say that?

Cathy cleared the table, went inside and loaded the dishwasher. Then she placed a slice of pie on a plate and joined her father, who had moved to the living room.

"Any plans for tonight?" he asked.

"I need to write another two thousand words for today, so I'll probably focus on that. Is that okay?"

Her father shrugged. "I have enough to keep me busy. I'm working on a few projects for you and a manuscript for another author."

Cathy was thrilled to see him branching out and freelancing for other writers. It gave him a challenge, and writers always needed someone who knew how to format manuscripts properly.

Now if only I could finish the thriller...

It wasn't writer's block that was getting in the way—she didn't believe in it. What prevented her from working on the thriller was a new horror novella plot that had slithered into shape, gripping her mind with sharp claws that wouldn't let go. She *had* to write the novella, and with the mood she was currently in, the horror genre beckoned with a combination of anticipation, excitement and trepidation.

* * *

Two hours later, she took a break and made some coffee. It wasn't until she sat back down again that she recalled the annoying house pest in the cupboard. "Dad, did you check the mouse traps?"

"Didn't even think about it. I'll do it now." He stood, stretched then wandered into the kitchen. A minute later, he called out, "No mouse. And no fresh turds." He returned to the sofa and sat, setting the laptop tray across his thighs.

The house grew silent, and the minutes ticked by.

She was working on a gruesome scene when a blur of motion caught her eye. She glanced down at the floor just in time to see a gray shadow slip under the couch, inches from her father's feet. She opened her mouth to say something to him then gritted her teeth. *Did I imagine that?*

She stared at the spot for several minutes, but nothing moved.

Don't be so silly! There's nothing there.

She sank into the recliner, determined to continue writing, but before she could hit one key, a gray streak raced across the floor and darted beneath the dining room table.

"Ah!" Cathy shouted, lifting her bare feet off the floor. "Mouse!"

With a groan of dread, she leapt onto the sofa. "Sorry, Dad. I can't stand that it's running around us." She started to laugh. "Oh God, this is so ridiculous. First the spiders, now a mouse? What the hell is next? A frickin' tarantula?"

"I'll be right back," her father said.

"Wait! Where are you going? Don't leave me here with this beast." She grinned when he peered over his shoulder at her. "Seriously, I don't do well with rodents running around my feet. Ew..." She waved clenched fists in the air.

In all honesty, she expected Lars, former military spy, to look at her with sheer disdain and perhaps a touch of shame. She was acting weak, and she knew it. But her reaction came from past experiences—and not positive ones. These phobias had appeared when she was a young child and had continued growing since then, and they weren't prepared to let her go. Not yet.

"I'm getting a broom," he said in a calm voice. "I'll be right back."

When her father reappeared holding a flimsy kitchen broom, Cathy blew out a measured breath and made a beeline for the dining room. She sat down, grabbing a second chair and sliding it closer so she could rest her feet on it.

"Whatever you do, Dad, please don't send it this way."

"I'll get him, Cathy."

The next twenty minutes reminded her of 1970s slapstick comedy shows. In the ever-darkening room, her father hopped around the room, bashing the hardwood floor with the broom every time the mouse poked its head from the shadows. Not once did the broom bristles make contact with the rodent.

In a low voice she said, "Lars Kilborn, AKA Double-Oh-Zero, at your service."

Her father snorted. "Don't be a smartass."

The mouse streaked past his feet, and Cathy let out a squeal. "Get him!"

Whack!

He missed again.

"Come on, Dad! You can do it. Smack the little bastard!"

The mouse retreated under the sofa.

Then all went quiet.

Her father stood motionless, the broom frozen in place over his head. Cathy held her breath. Her pulse quickened as she wiped sweaty palms on her pants.

"There he is," her father said. "By the fireplace."

"Now it's under the loveseat. Wait! It ran back under the sofa."

The little shit kept darting back and forth between the two pieces of furniture. It was a wonder her father wasn't dizzy. However, he was slowing down.

"Okay, take a break, Dad," she said. "I don't think the broom's helping."

With a shrug, he headed into the dining room and took a chair next to her.

"How are we gonna catch this thing?" she asked, eyes glued to the last place she'd seen the furry pest.

"I don't know."

She scowled. "I bet it's watching us right now, laughing at us."

"He probably is. He thinks he's invincible."

With a roll of her eyes, Cathy gave her father a bleak smile. "You're a lot of help. You're supposed to save your daughter. You know, like Liam Neeson always does in his movies."

"Except we're not in a movie. And I'm not Liam Neeson."

She gave him a sweet smile. "So you're not gonna save your only daughter from the mouse apocalypse? We could be his next meal. Especially since the traps are in the cupboards, and he's out here."

Her father sighed. "Let's put them in the middle of the living room. That way, we'll see him go inside, and I'll dispose of him tonight."

"Okay. I'll get the traps."

With the spin traps placed in the center of the living room carpet, they sat mere yards away, watching and waiting.

It didn't take long.

Drawn by the scent of peanut butter bait, the mouse materialized from beneath the loveseat. It took tentative steps closer, its nose wriggling. Every few steps, it would stop, sit on its haunches and stare in their direction.

"Jesus," Cathy whispered. "It *is* watching us."

With the rodent frozen in place, she took the opportunity to study it, though she couldn't see much definition in the looming darkness of the room. The creature's gray fur and dark, beady eyes gave it an ominous appearance. It didn't look anything like the white mice she'd seen in pet stores. This one wasn't overly large. It would fit in the palm of her hand—if she were crazy enough to hold it. And that wasn't about to happen any time soon. *Or ever!*

Now she remembered why she hated mice. They always looked ravenous, like they'd eat anything, including humans. It was a ridiculous thought, but that's where her mind went.

Eat the frickin' bait!

When the mouse finally moved, it walked away from the traps.

Cathy groaned. "No…come on. This is gonna take all night."

The mouse twitched, almost as though it had heard her. Then it turned back.

"That's it," she murmured, her heart racing with anticipation. "I hope the little bastard takes the bait."

The mouse inched its way closer to one of the chunks of black plastic in the middle of the carpet. Then "the little bastard" stuck its head inside the trap entrance and licked at a tiny smear of peanut butter.

"Go *in*side," Cathy said between clenched teeth.

Again, the rodent's head disappeared into the opening, and once more it backed away from the trap, unharmed.

She yawned. "This is taking forever, Dad, and we both need to go to bed."

A terrible thought struck her. What if they didn't catch the stupid thing? What if "the little bastard" was still running around the house when she went to bed? How was she ever going to sleep?

"Yeah, he's not cooperating," her father said. "We could be up all night waiting for him to enter a trap. The good thing is he knows where they are now, and he obviously likes peanut butter."

"You think we should call it a night?"

He nodded. "Maybe he'll feel more comfortable when we're gone."

She considered this for a moment. Perhaps her father was right.

She shuddered. "Only one problem…"

"What's that?"

"Whoever built this house left an inch and a half gap at the bottom of every door." She pointed to the guest room door. "See? That mouse would have no problem ducking underneath."

"We could block those gaps with something like—"

"Towels!"

Within minutes, bath and hand towels were stuffed under the doors, leaving Cathy's bedroom and the guest room for last.

"Okay, Dad, I'm going to bed. See you in the morning."

"Goodnight, Cathy."

With a backward glance at the traps, she said a quick prayer of thanks that her father had decided to drop by and stay overnight. He'd been surprisingly supportive, and she made a mental note to thank him in the morning.

She slid beneath the sheets and reached for the apnea mask. She examined the nose piece. *No spiders.* For good measure she turned on the machine and listened to the hiss of air. If anything *had* climbed inside, the air pressure would spit it out.

She slipped the mask over her head, securing it over her nose and doing her best not to imagine bugs squirming inside the hose. Turning on her side, she eyed the towel under the door and thought of the mouse. God forbid it managed to squeeze itself past the towel and into the bedroom.

A panic attack set in, and she struggled to slow her breathing.

I'm suffocating!

She ripped off the mask and lunged forward in bed, her breathing labored, as though the room lacked any oxygen. This had happened a few times, mainly early on when she'd first been put on the CPAP machine. Eventually, the moment would pass.

In…out…in…out…

When the attack was over, she readjusted the mask and took measured breaths. She tapped the light and was plunged into darkness.

Thinking about the day's ordeals, it was difficult not to feel somewhat silly and embarrassed when she replayed everything in her head. Her father probably thought she'd overreacted. Mike would, too.

Yes, she was a wimp when it came to insects and rodents. The thought of bugs on her skin made her shiver in fear.

Lying in bed, she remembered why…

Chapter 6
"Wings of a Butterfly"

Lice. Her bug phobia had started with head lice.

Back when Cathy was in elementary school in the remote town of Masset on the Queen Charlotte Islands, those disgusting bugs had infested the heads of many of her classmates. Students were often reminded not to share brushes or combs. Teachers warned everyone not to share hats or scarves, too. They'd even had a nurse come in occasionally to comb through students' hair.

Cathy liked the nurse's visits. Every time one of her friends played with her hair, it sent a pleasant quiver up her spine. Her friends felt the same, so it wasn't unusual to see one braiding another's hair, or using one of their own elastic bands to secure their model's ponytail. That was probably how the outbreak had started.

In all honesty, she hadn't paid much attention to the whole lice thing. She was a kid. Nothing like that would ever happen to her. She was invincible.

Or so she'd thought.

At eight years old, she'd been blessed with thick reddish-brown hair, though some days she'd didn't see it as anything other than a curse. She was teased mercilessly for being a typical "ginger," though they didn't use that term back in the olden days. "Carrot Head" and "Freckle Face" were popular then, and she'd been labeled both.

One day after school she decided to wash her hair in the bathroom sink. All day long she'd experienced a weird, fluttery sensation all over her scalp, as though the wings of a butterfly were lightly brushing against her hair. She couldn't stop scratching. Still, she never once thought of lice—until she raised her shampoo-soaked head and saw dozens of pale, *live* bugs squirming in the sink. Revolted by the sight, she cried out for her mother.

"Help me!" Sobbing hysterically, Cathy pulled at her hair. "Get these bugs off me! Get them off!"

Not even Margot, with her warm embrace and calm words, could soothe Cathy. What could she say? The revulsion in her mother's eyes said it all as she warily wrapped a towel around Cathy's head. "I'll go buy some lice shampoo. Stay here in the bathroom. Don't go anywhere, Cathy."

With no other choice, her mother disappeared, leaving a hysterical eight-year-old to deal with writhing insects in the sink, on the floor and in her hair. Terrified, Cathy scraped at her scalp with her fingers and ripped out handfuls of hair in the process.

That day she learned the definition of "forever." It had taken *forever* for her mother to return. And no matter how hard she tried, she couldn't stop thinking about the invasion crawling all over her skin.

Before that day, she hadn't thought much about insects. She'd even held ladybugs in her hand, watching their yellow trails cross her palm. What was there about the small, red bugs that made them seem harmless and fun?

Fun? What the hell had she been thinking?

A couple of years later, in junior high, she'd studied the "bugs," only to discover they weren't technically insects but beetles. She also learned the yellowish stain wasn't urine but a bloodlike fluid called hemolymph. Ladybugs secreted hemolymph from their leg joints as a defense against predators that were either repelled by the noxious odor or toxins prevalent in some ladybug species. Yet, Cathy endured the yellow stains on her hands and the stink because she'd thought ladybugs were "cute." However, there was no way she'd endure lice squirming around in her hair.

When her mother finally returned, she washed Cathy's hair three times with foul-smelling shampoo. Years later, her mother admitted she'd even considered chopping off Cathy's long red locks. Cathy would have preferred a close shave.

Her phobia for bugs touching her body started that terrible day. Traumatized by the experience, she'd had nightmares for months, and she'd become petrified of the dark. It took years to wipe her mind clean of the memory of vicious lice biting her flesh and wriggling all over her scalp.

Thinking about it now made her entire head itch.

Chapter 7
"Walk Away"

Eager to start Sunday off positively, Cathy poured coffee into a mug and turned on her laptop. She was surprised she'd slept, particularly with the bottom of the bedroom door jammed up with a towel. Right before she'd fallen asleep, her anxiety had kicked in.

What if the house caught fire and someone had to get into my room? The towel would make that difficult.

"Cathy," her father called out. "I'm heading home now."

"Okay, Dad. Thanks again. Especially for trying to catch the mouse."

"You'll be fine."

"I know. And Mike's on his way home."

She walked her father to the door, gave him a hug and watched him climb into his car. After he was gone, she sat outside on the deck, sipping coffee and watching for birds.

Excitement and relief welled in her heart. Mike would be home in mere minutes, and he'd promised to buy some poison and take care of the mouse situation. He was her savior. Her hero.

She let out a soft laugh, followed by a long, slow breath. "It's only a mouse. It could be worse. Hell, the spiders were worse. So were the flies and maggots. One mouse? How much trouble could it be?"

"You talking to me?" someone shouted.

When she stood, she saw her neighbor, Les, near their shared fence. She waved. "How's everything?"

"All good here, but I'm not sure talking to yourself is a sane thing to do."

She laughed. "Don't worry. I talk to myself all the time. Just ask Mike. It helps me focus, especially when problem-solving."

"So what's the problem?"

"A frickin' mouse."

"Did you buy traps?"

"Yeah, but the mouse doesn't seem interested. Damned thing ran all around the living room, ignoring the traps or walking around them. I think it was laughing at us."

"When does Mike get back?"

She looked at her watch. "Any minute now. Thank God. Then we can call him 'Mike the Mouse Hunter.'"

Les gave a nod. "Well, happy hunting." He disappeared into the shed in his backyard.

Cathy finished her coffee. Heading inside, she heard a groaning sound coming from the pantry. It took her a minute to realize it was the garage door.

Mike was home.

Her husband peered around the corner. "Hi, honey, I'm ho-ome."

She ran into his arms and kissed him. "I've really missed you."

"Sure you have." His grip tightened around her. "You just want me for my mouse-killing superpowers."

"That, too." She grinned up at him. "You get that little bastard, and I'll give you a reward later."

Mike grinned. "Promises, promises."

"I want that mouse gone. One way or the other."

He kissed her. "No more talk of rodents. I've missed you—phobias and all."

After a quick coffee and chat to catch up, Mike drove to Home Depot and picked up mouse poison, the kind that dehydrated rodents until they shriveled up into dust. At least that's how Mike explained it.

Once the bait was set in the cupboards, they drove across the bridge to Kelowna.

"How about lunch at Lord Chumley's?" she suggested.

"Sounds good to me."

Lord Chumley's Fish & Chips was a popular little restaurant known for its English-style batter and home fries. Tracy, the owner, always made a point of chatting with her customers and getting to know them—another benefit of living in a small town. Tracy could spot a newbie coming in the door. That was exactly what happened the first time Cathy and her mother dined there.

"How have you two been?" Tracy asked, approaching their table.

"Mike just got home."

"Oh? Where'd they send you this time? The middle of nowhere?"

Mike nodded. "Northern BC."

Tracy smiled at Cathy. "Bet you're glad he's back."

"You have no idea."

"That sounds ominous. What's up?"

"She thinks our house is infested with spiders and mice," Mike said.

"Don't forget flies and maggots," Cathy added.

"Yuck," Tracy said. "That's not good. Did you call an exterminator?"

Mike grinned. "*I'm* the exterminator. The *Mike*-enator."

Everyone laughed.

"Well, here's your food," Tracy said as a server approached with two plates of lightly battered halibut and fries. "I'll talk to you later. Enjoy your lunch."

"We will," Cathy said.

After Tracy left, Mike leaned across the table. "Want me to help you with that *infestation* of fries."

Cathy smacked his arm. "Wiseass."

For all his teasing, he made her laugh. He was the sunshine on her rainy days, which were far more often now that they lived in BC.

"What are you thinking?" he asked.

"That I'll stay here for the day while you exterminate."

He sighed. "The bait I bought can take up to a week to work."

"What?" She moaned softly. "I was hoping this would be a quick fix. Like *today*."

"Takes time."

"As long as we can stuff a towel under the door at night."

* * *

To take her mind off dying rodents, Cathy took her laptop out to the deck when they returned home. The horror novella was coming along nicely. She'd set up the characters and the major plot points, and the chapters were practically writing themselves. She loved it when an idea took off and everything fell neatly into place.

Writing horror had one catch, though. It made her more paranoid.

A fly zoomed past her face, and she jerked backward. She grabbed the laptop just in time to prevent it from sliding off the tray.

She scratched her head. Her hand froze as it brought back visions of lice.

Think of something else.

A shiver trickled up her spine, and she glanced at the sliding door behind her. An army-green stink bug took cautious steps across the glass, its body resembling a miniature military tank—armor and all. Watching it sent a shudder of dread up her back, and her fingernails raked red marks into her skin.

Seconds passed.

She snatched the fly swatter from the hook on the stucco then squished the stink bug with one hard smack. *Mother Nature, be damned.*

"You better hope he didn't have any family," Mike teased from the doorway. "They might be looking for payback, a little divine retribution."

"Stop it. That's not funny."

"You can't kill every insect in the world."

"I know. We need them for some ungodly reason, or the earth does. The circle of life. Blah, blah, blah."

"I'm going down to my 'Man Cave' to watch the race." At the top of the stairs, he paused. "Do you have supper plans?"

"Yeah, baked mouse with mashed stink bugs and spider salad, followed by maggot mousse for dessert." Her mouth turned down in distaste. "Ugh, I shouldn't have said that."

Laughter rumbled through the house as Mike disappeared downstairs.

Returning to the horror novella, Cathy pounded out another two thousand words then decided to pack it in. This was her husband's first day home after a week away, and she wanted to make it special, not ignore him all day long.

I'll make one of his favorites—spaghetti with meat sauce, Caesar salad and garlic toast.

In the kitchen, she dumped sauce ingredients into the crockpot and sautéed a package of lean ground beef and fresh garlic. An onion, green pepper and mushrooms were next. She added the meat and vegetable mix to the pot. A splash or two of her homemade sherry pepper sauce gave the meat sauce a spicy bite, and fresh oregano and basil from the pots on her deck were the final touch. While the sauce simmered, she puttered around the kitchen, preparing the salad and garlic toast.

"Red wine will go nicely with supper."

She kept liquor in the corner cabinet—the one with the missing lazy Susan shelves. As she reached for a bottle of wine, that's when she remembered the mouse. With a sheepish chuckle, she selected a bottle of Damitz Good Red Wine, made by an Okanagan winery she and Mike had discovered while touring Lake Country.

A flicker of movement flashed in the back of the cabinet.

The mouse?

Chewing her bottom lip, Cathy peered into the cupboard and nudged one of the bottles. Her mind conjured up images of a sharp-clawed, rabid-looking rodent lunging for her face, its teeth dripping with blood. She waited for the scurrying of tiny feet, but nothing moved. Using a wooden spoon, she gingerly moved the bottles to the side so she could see the back wall of the cabinet.

No mouse. Maybe she'd imagined it.

Don't be so paranoid.

* * *

"I know we said we'd wait a few years," she said as they climbed into bed, "but I think we should start looking for properties and build our dream home now."

Mike frowned. "Why? There's nothing wrong with this house."

"How can you say that? It's been one headache after another. For me, anyway. I keep waiting for the next bomb to drop, the next invasion of God-only-knows-what, and I can't stop wondering what we did to deserve such bad luck."

Mike gathered her into his arms. "We didn't do anything. I realize you've had some unpleasant experiences here, but we're fortunate to live the lives we have. Especially you. Not everyone gets the chance to do what they dream."

"I get that—really I do. But this is starting to feel more like a nightmare."

"You're letting your phobias get to you."

She turned away. *That's what I'm afraid of. That they'll get me.*

Before he turned out the light, Mike added, "Don't forget, Cathy, you killed the spiders, got rid of the flies and maggots and the mouse will be dead soon. We're the lucky ones."

"Then why do I feel like our luck is about to run out?"

* * *

An intricate web of interconnecting tunnels was carved deep within the walls of the house and beneath the ground surrounding it. It lurked in one of the tunnels, listening to the humans squawking at each other. It waited with great patience for the most opportune time—and that time was coming.

Soon…

Chapter 8
"I Will Not Bow"

On Wednesday, Mike headed out of town again, this time only for three days. Cathy could survive that long without him. They had caught the mouse, after all. In fact, Mike told her he'd found two carcasses behind the fridge. The rodents had taken the bait, and that was that.

Dead mice walking.

"What are your plans?" Mike asked when he called her that day.

"I'm going to spend the weekend writing and doing laundry." *Probably mostly writing.*

She managed to get a load of darks into the washing machine before succumbing to the tantalizing lure of the novella. There was something about this story that excited her. She had a feeling her fans were in for a creepy-crawly treat.

She sat on the recliner in the living room, her laptop on a tray, and worked on the novella. Hours passed in what seemed like minutes. When she eventually looked up, the room was in shadows, and it wasn't even six o'clock.

"Aw, crap."

Outside, a storm simmered. The sky turned from white to pale gray and then to a gloomy slate. Within minutes the sky was a maelstrom of churning air and dank humidity. A streak of lightning flashed across the sky on the other side of the lake above Kelowna, followed twenty seconds later by a low rumble. It was odd how the bad weather seemed to always hit that side and not West Kelowna.

Cathy stood in the doorway to the deck and counted the seconds between lightning and thunder. Fourteen seconds this time. The storm was moving closer.

She took a step back and something small and dark on the hardwood floor caught her eye. An ant.

She stepped on it with her slipper. "This is *my* home, buddy."

Her stomach growled. *Suppertime.*

She cranked up the music to drown out the pounding rain and booming thunder and headed into the kitchen where she began to prepare a feta Caesar salad. As she reached for bacon bits in the fridge drawer, movement on the floor made her look down. "What the hell?"

Ants walked single file from beneath the refrigerator.

Cathy backed away, startled by the sight. She counted them. An even dozen.

A shiver of dread tricked down her spine. *What if there's a nest behind the fridge and they just hatched...or whatever ants do?*

There was no way in hell she was moving the refrigerator to find out. With her joint condition, she couldn't, even if she wanted to. Which she definitely didn't.

"Okay, Cathy," she mumbled. "You can do this. A few ants are nothing."

She strode out to the deck and grabbed the fly swatter she kept on a hook. Armed with the deadly weapon, she returned to the kitchen and discovered the ants had split up in multiple directions. *Little bastards.*

She spent the next few minutes squishing as many ants as she could and disposing of their bodies down the sink drain. She hit the garbage disposal button for good measure.

They'd never had ant problems in Edmonton, or anywhere else for that matter, and she didn't know much about them, but their size disturbed her. They weren't the small black ants she was used to seeing outside. These were black with red in the middle part of their body.

Carpenter ants?

She'd heard that carpenter ants were like termites, destructive and hard to get rid of, but she wasn't sure what they looked like, so she did a quick Google search. Within minutes she learned more than she wanted about the pests. Carpenter ants were carnivorous insects, often feeding off the remains of other bugs or ants. They didn't *eat* wood; carpenter ants chewed through wood to create intricate tunnels and nesting areas, and their bite contained a toxin that could be irritating to humans or pets. The photos matched the ants she'd killed.

"Why does this always happen when you're out of town?" she said when Mike called after supper.

"Did you put some ant bait down?"

"Yes. I slid two tins underneath the fridge."

"Chances are you killed them all, but let me know if you see any more."

* * *

That evening, after a productive day of writing, Cathy indulged in a little binge watching of season three of *One Tree Hill*. After the third episode, she decided to treat herself to some ice cream.

She took two steps into the kitchen and jolted to a stop. Seven ants scurried across the floor, inches from her bare feet. Out came the fly swatter, and down went the bodies into the sink drain.

She recalled something she'd read. "You're nocturnal hunters."

Shining a small flashlight under the refrigerator, she saw the two tins of ant bait. She used a wooden spoon to sweep them out into the middle of the floor. Since ants hunted for food at night, it would be better to have the tins where she could see them.

Standing at a distance, she watched and waited.

She didn't wait long.

A large, bulbous-bodied ant appeared from beneath the fridge. It was followed closely by a second, somewhat smaller, ant. They meandered over to one of the tins.

She crossed her fingers. "Eat."

The ants walked around the tin for a few agonizing minutes before heading off in the opposite direction.

Cathy groaned. "Come on. Eat the bait."

If they took the bait back to the nest, the entire colony would die. That was the plan, anyway.

After ten minutes of waiting, she swatted the duo and sent them down the drain. Seconds after she'd disposed of them, three more ants climbed up the lower cabinet doors.

Swat! Swat! Swat!

As she turned to leave, another ant caught her eye. This one was on the fridge door handle. *Ugh.*

SWAT!

Three steps around the island and she spotted another ant on the counter by the sink. It met its watery grave within seconds.

She stood there, slowly turning in a circle, her gaze sweeping across the cabinets, doors, counters and floor. Ants materialized from every nook and cranny, as though conjured by dark magic.

With a small moan, she attacked every speck with the swatter, sending a few innocent crumbs flying. "Great, now I'm feeding these pests."

When the kitchen was finally clear, Cathy released a pent-up breath and examined the wasteland. Tiny body parts littered the hardwood, and she spent the next half hour vacuuming the floor and scrubbing the counters.

Mike would be proud.

* * *

Mike arrived home on Friday night, but there were no tantalizing smells coming from the kitchen, and that could only mean one thing.

"We're ordering out," Cathy said when he entered the living room.

"I figured as much. How'd it go with the ant issue?"

"We've got a real problem here. I've found the fuckers on the fridge, counters, in the sink and all over the floor. Spent the last two days swatting ants and itching and scratching like crazy." She peered over her eyeglasses at him. "So, all in all, not a good day."

"I can't see any now."

"Of course you can't. They come out at night when it's dark."

She turned on every light around them.

"What are you doing, Cathy?"

"Ants are nocturnal. They come out mainly at night. To *feed*. And I don't want them feeding on us."

He strode around the house, turning out lights as he passed by. "We're trying to conserve energy."

She could tell by his clamped lips and eye rolling that Mike wasn't impressed. She gritted her teeth and tamped down a snarky reply. Sure, she could be overdramatic sometimes. It was part of her charm. But he didn't have to brush off her fears as though they were nothing. What did he need—the cupboards to cave in before he believed her?

Retribution was about five minutes away.

"And there we go," she said. "Look at that."

"What?"

"The ants go marching one by one," she sang, her tone full of sarcasm. "Across the wall. Four of them." She nodded her head toward the dining room wall.

"It'll take a week or so for the bait to work." He gave her a sheepish smile. "I'll take care of these four. You go sit down and relax."

"Relax? Fucking ants are everywhere, Mike. One made me break a mug. I tried to swat it before it got inside the cupboard. I knocked the mug out instead, and it shattered everywhere."

"Did you get the ant?"

"No. It's still in the cupboard somewhere, and I'm not going in after it. I've killed over three dozen ants a day since this started. I'm so sick of all the bugs in this house. It's been one after the other."

"Cathy, calm down. You killed the spiders, we haven't seen a mouse since the first two and there are no more flies and maggots in the garage, now that I've built the trash shed outside."

"You left out the ants."

"A few dozen ants, oh well." He shrugged. "Our house isn't infested."

She gaped at him. *Why won't you listen?* "Something is very wrong with this house, Mike. Every day I wait for some other *infestation* to hit us. Frogs, maybe. Or locusts, or wasps."

"Now you're just being silly."

"Maybe. But what if I'm right?"

"Then we'll deal with it when necessary. If we have to do home renovations, fine. Give me a few more months, and I'll start working on some of these projects." The intense frustration she'd felt diminished with each word Mike said. "We can rip open the kitchen—extend the island like you wanted—and I'll make sure everything is clean, inside and out."

"Can you start with that cupboard right there? That's the one the ant is in."

Mike drew out a long, exaggerated sigh. "Yes, dear. I'm on it."

"You're the best. I love you."

* * *

Small black eyes witnessed the senseless murder of its fellow tunnel travelers. Hatred gathered under its fur and seeped into its small bones.

The humans had to go, and it would do anything to make that happen.

Humans—a scourge upon the earth.

It scurried deeper into the tunnel. It would not rest until their home had been purged.

Time to eliminate these pests…

Chapter 9
"Crawling"

Mike spent Saturday morning pulling all the appliances out of the kitchen and checking for ants or debris left from their chewing. Other than two small holes in the wall, he saw no signs of damage or pests.

"I can't tell where they came from," he told Cathy. "Maybe we finally got them all."

By that evening they were once again dodging ants on the floor.

Cathy let out a soft wail. "They're on the ceiling now."

When he glanced up, Mike saw five ants crawling upside down across the living room ceiling. One took a misstep and fell to the floor where he stepped on it.

"Where the hell are they coming from?"

" *'Hell'* might be the operative word there," she muttered.

Mike wandered outside and placed a few ant bait tins around the exterior walls of the house. Nothing stood out as being a problem.

So how are these ants getting inside?

He found Cathy in the pantry off the kitchen. Cheap brown melamine shelves had been built along the right wall, the shelves overcrowded with various grocery items and oversized pots and bowls. A stainless steel LG washer/dryer set lined the back wall, and previous owners had added a white-painted wood shelf above the appliances.

"I didn't see any obvious entrance outside," he said, "but then again, we're talking little ants here."

"What about this closet?"

To the left of the door leading out to the garage was a narrow door to a small broom closet with three upper shelves. They stored lightbulbs and flashlights on the shelves, and two plastic bins for recycling cans and bottles sat on the floor.

Mike had taken a quick peek inside earlier, but with no sign of ants anywhere in the pantry, he'd dismissed the closet as being the culprit.

"I'll take everything out and check again."

"I'm making grilled cheese for lunch. You want to eat now or after the closet?"

He arched a brow. "What do *you* think?"

"Lunch, it is."

Ripping the house apart wasn't his idea of a relaxing day off, but Mike's inner intellectual reminded him of the price they'd paid for the house. One had to keep on top of problematic house pests; otherwise he and Cathy would be run out of their home.

After a quick bite to eat, he made his way back to the pantry. As well as the two recycle bins, Cathy had stuffed a Swiffer sweeper, a mop and an extendable dust brush into the angled corner. Once he'd cleared out the space, he discovered the closet was bigger than he'd thought.

He stuck his head inside. *Ah, crap.*

Whoever had built the house had forgotten to tape and mud the interior corner of the closet. Where the two walls butted, there was a three-foot-long gap that ran down to the floor, and a dozen or more black bodies swarmed around the gap.

"Cathy, I found more ants!"

His wife appeared in the doorway. "In the closet?"

He nodded. "You can't see all the way into the corner unless you take everything out and step inside. And now I see where they've been hiding during the day, and you can bet there's a nest in there, too."

"You mean to tell me they're in the wall? Ugh."

He frowned. "The empty pop and beer cans must have attracted them to the area."

With the fly swatter in hand, he cleared off the wall. Four fat ants escaped into the void behind the wall, and he prayed these weren't pregnant queens. He slid a bait tin into the gap, wishing it didn't take so long to kill the buggers.

One week...

Two stupid ants climbed out of the hole just in time to get whacked.

* * *

By Wednesday, Cathy and Mike were still finding ants—live *and* dead ones—all over the kitchen and living room.

After lunch, Mike went downstairs to play Rock Band. His virtual band, The Mike-enators, was in the top ten percent on the leaderboard, and he was crushing it on lead guitar.

But in his man cave, he realized carpenter ants weren't as stupid as he'd thought. They were now migrating downstairs. He picked up at least a dozen bodies embedded in the carpet and flushed them down the toilet.

Later, when he told Cathy, she was horrified. "Mom will be back in four days, and there's no way she can handle this. I think it's time to call someone in."

"You're right. I'll take care of it."

"While you're in ass-kicking superhero mode, can you take a look at *that*?" She indicated a shadow on the vaulted living room ceiling. "I think that blob is a spider."

"Nah, it's too big," Mike argued. "Probably just a piece of dust."

Cathy eyed the ceiling. "I don't know…"

"Why don't you go have a bath, while I make the appointment for an exterminator to come in?"

"You're too good to me."

"That's what superheroes are for. You can pay me back later." He smiled suggestively, and Cathy giggled all the way to the bedroom.

Google located a company in Kelowna called The Bugman Pest Control Services, and Mike dialed the number. He was particularly curious about whether they needed to evacuate the premises during the service.

"Not with our product," the receptionist said. "We spray a liquid neurotoxin on your baseboards. We can have someone out there this afternoon."

"The sooner, the better," Mike replied. "Preferably *before* my wife books a five-star hotel for the week."

An hour later, Bugman Mitch Williams showed up in a pale yellow Volkswagen Beetle. Mike followed him around while Mitch sprayed all the baseboards, upstairs and down, plus the gap in the broom closet and the attic over the kitchen.

"It's pet and people friendly," Mitch assured him.

"The only pets we have are spiders, mice, flies and maggots."

Mitch raised a brow. "Oh? How long have you lived here?"

"Not even a year." Mike filled the exterminator in on the problems they'd experienced *and* Cathy's bug phobia.

"Well, we do get bugs here," Mitch said. "It's kind of the price you pay for living in paradise. But it does sound like an abnormal amount of house pests over a short duration of time."

"I think we have everything under control now, except these ants."

"I'll take care of those for you. We'll do one more interior treatment in about a month and three treatments outside your home over the next few months. Our goal is to destroy the entire colony before the head queen feels threatened and disperses other queens to repopulate in new areas of your house."

"We're finding really big ants in the basement now—*live* ones. Do you think the queens are re-establishing more nests?"

Mitch shrugged. "Could be. But don't worry. Eventually they'll make contact with the baseboards. But be warned—you may see increased activity over the next few days. Then you'll find more dead ants."

"Oh joy. Cathy won't be happy to hear that."

"But I bet she'll be happy when there aren't any ants crawling around your home."

"Yes, she will."

Chapter 10
"Electric Love"

Two days after the Bugman's visit, Cathy received a call from Mike, who was working in Penticton that week. "My supervisor just informed me I'll only be working in the Kelowna/Penticton area moving forward, now that the northern BC project is finished."

Relief swept over her as she sank into a chair in the dining room. "That's awesome news."

"I figured you could use some good news for a change. How's the ant situation?"

"I found a couple of dead ones this morning, but that's it."

"No live ones?"

"Not a one." She smiled. "Finally, a reprieve."

"So all is quiet on the home front."

"Well…maybe not all. Remember that big blob on the ceiling? The one I thought was a spider?"

"Yeah. What about it?"

"It's gone now."

"Good."

"Not really. It could be anywhere."

"So now you can find it and kill it."

"Ha ha. I don't know where it is. And sending me to find a spider is like sending in the woman with the dying flashlight in a horror movie." She paused for effect. "And in case you don't know how *that* ends, she doesn't survive."

"You can do it," Mike said, his voice sounding hundreds of miles away. "You're no ordinary woman. You're more than that."

She laughed. "What are you drinking?"

"Coffee."

"When will you be home?"

"I should be there around six."

"Okay. I'll marinate some steaks for supper."

"Sounds great. All I've had to eat so far today is a bag of chips."

"Mike, you can't live off junk food."

"I know." She could tell he was grinning when he said, "But I can try."

She hung up and was about to make another call when a noise made her jump. Someone else was in the house.

Break-in!

She grabbed the nearest object as a weapon, her handbag. She held it high above her head by the straps as she quietly edged toward the foyer.

"Cathy! What are you doing?"

Her father stood by the front door, a mix of surprise and shock on his weathered face.

With a breathless giggle, she lowered the handbag. "Jesus, you scared the crap out of me, Dad."

"Sorry, I was looking for lightbulbs."

She gaped at him. "But what are you doing here? I didn't hear your car pull up."

"It's in the shop. I blew a tire on the drive up."

"So you took a cab here to change my lightbulbs."

He laughed. "I had an appointment in town. Now I'm waiting for the tire to be fixed. Since I had time to kill, I figured I take care of the pool chemicals for you."

"I thought someone had broken in. I almost clobbered you."

"With *that*?" He indicated her handbag.

She gave him a sheepish grin. "It was the first thing I grabbed."

"Oh, I forgot to tell you, I found this on the floor in the storage room earlier." He handed her a ladies glove. It looked vaguely familiar.

"It's not mine," she said, setting the glove on her mother's coffee table. "Must be Mom's."

As they made their way upstairs, her father said, "My car should be ready soon, and then I'll be out of your hair. I'll go do the pool chemicals now. "

"Thanks, Dad. I appreciate it."

She glanced at the clock on the microwave. It was nearly 2:00 p.m.

"Dad," she called. "I'm going to give my neighbor a call. Her dogs are missing, and I want to find out if she found them. I might go visit her."

"Okay. I'll probably be gone before you get back."

"No worries. I have a dentist appointment in an hour and a half anyway."

Cathy searched for the note with Ellen Wichman's number and found it taped to the side of the fridge.

Ellen picked up after four rings. "What do *you* want?"

"I, uh, was hoping we could get together for quick coffee."

"Really. Coffee." Ellen's voice was spiked with sarcasm. "Maybe I'll consider that if you tell me what you did with my babies."

"Huh?"

"Don't 'huh' me. I know you did something to Molly and Roxanne."

About four months ago, Ellen had moved into a two-story home three doors down. Cathy had first noticed her while picking up mail from the community box a block away. It was hard *not* to notice her. Ellen was wearing a floppy red hat, and two curly-haired gray poodles walked beside her—off leash.

Cathy blew out a breath. "Your dogs."

"Of course I mean my dogs."

"I haven't seen them since you let them out last weekend. Why do you think I have your dogs? If they've gone missing, they could be anywhere by now."

"I found their collars, all covered in mud, on your front lawn this morning."

"Just their collars?" *That's weird.*

"I've seen you looking at my babies when we walk past your house. You don't like them. And why else would their collars be on *your* lawn if you didn't do something to them?"

"That's not true. I wouldn't hurt them. I love dogs." *Just not your yappy poodles that you allow to run loose and poop on other people's lawns.*

"If Roxanne and Molly aren't back here by tomorrow morning, I'm calling the police. You hear me?" Ellen slammed down the phone.

Cathy frowned. *What the heck was that all about?*

Opening the front door, she stepped outside and strolled around the yard, searching for any sign of Ellen's dogs. A small, semi-moist turd under the maple tree indicated someone's dog had relieved itself on her grass sometime in the past day. With a huff of irritation, she went back inside for some paper towel, and when she returned, she scooped up the poop and disposed of it in the trash bin.

An inspection of the bushes came next.

Sunlight bounced off something small and shiny underneath a rose bush.

"What's this?" She leaned down. "Molly's ID tag."

She flipped over the small heart-shaped dog tag. A dried crimson streak covered Ellen's address. *Blood!*

"Uh-oh. This can't be good."

A thorough search of the front yard yielded no new evidence. Ellen's dogs had been in her yard, no doubt about that. The woman had said she'd found both collars but that they'd been muddy.

Standing with hands on hips, Cathy surveyed her yard and the street. Dogs went missing all the time, usually a result of bear or other animal attacks. They did live in the BC mountains, after all.

Maybe that's what happened to Ellen's poodles. A bear got 'em.

Staring at the ID tag in her hand, she knew she'd have to talk to Ellen.

On the way to the woman's house, Cathy debated on how and what she'd say.

"Sorry, your dogs are probably dead," seemed way too harsh.

"Ellen, I found Molly's dog tag in the grass," she said instead. She handed Ellen the tag. "There's blood on the back. I think maybe a bear or coyote or cougar—"

"You're saying an animal killed my babies?" Ellen said, her eyes widening in dismay.

Cathy touched her arm. "We don't know that for sure. Maybe they got away."

"Then why didn't they come home?"

"Perhaps one of them is...injured. Or they just got lost. Have you called the SPCA?"

"Of course. They haven't seen Molly or Roxanne."

"You know, we once had a Siamese cat that climbed under the hood of my dad's car. When my dad started the engine, the cat freaked out and took off. We didn't see him for about a week. My parents thought he was dead. When he came home, he was missing his tail and one ear."

"That's awful, Cathy."

"Yeah. Except that he came home."

Ellen indicated a mud-caked mess on the small table by the door. "They had clean white collars, both of them. Where did all the mud come from?"

"Can I take a look?"

Ellen shrugged, and Cathy picked up the collars. She carefully pried off the dried mud, and bit by bit, the surface of each collar was exposed. The buckles were still fastened. What had once been white fabric was now stained a deep red.

More blood. Not a good sign.

Cathy handed the collars back to Ellen. "I hope you find your dogs." She glanced at her watch. "I have a dentist appointment to get to."

"If I find out you *do* have them…" The woman's mouth puckered in a scowl.

Cathy spun on one heel and strode back to her house and into the garage.

She'd done her neighborly duty. If Ellen wanted to accuse her, oh well.

* * *

Ellen squinted through the slats of the blinds and watched Cathy's car back out of the driveway. The car disappeared down the hill.

Donning a pair of leather driving gloves and a black jacket with a hood, she slipped out the front door and made her way to the Tremblays' house.

She didn't believe Cathy for a minute. The woman had given her babies the "evil eye" countless times, and Ellen was sure she'd find them locked in the basement or a back room.

She checked her watch. She had at least an hour. That would be more than enough time. And if she were wrong, Cathy would never know.

The street was quiet. The only movement was a faint breeze that swept over the trees. *Shhhhh...*

Ellen crept around the side of the house and opened the back gate. When she reached the back door, she said a quick prayer and pushed on the sliding door handle.

The door opened.

"Now we'll see who's lying."

The interior of the Tremblay home was hidden by gloomy shadows, and Ellen was afraid to turn on any lights. Last thing she wanted to do was alert other neighbors. And what if she forgot to turn them off? Cathy would know someone had broken in, and that would not end well for Ellen.

"Okay," she whispered. "Where are my babies?"

A soft creak came from somewhere in the house, and Ellen froze. Was someone else in the house? Did Cathy have company?

Silence.

She inched forward and climbed the stairs up to the main floor. A thorough sweep of every room upstairs produced nothing but frustration, and a little envy. The Tremblays had a substantial wine collection in the dining room.

"They won't miss one small bottle," Ellen murmured as she shoved a bottle of cabernet down the sleeve of her jacket.

Fifteen minutes later she realized her dogs were not upstairs.

"Well, that leaves the basement."

Ellen moved quietly down the stairs. The first room she checked was a family room, from the look of it. No place to hide her babies there.

A low groan echoed through the walls.

"Must have bad plumbing," she muttered.

Another sound, kind of like a yip or bark, came from inside the two-bedroom basement suite.

Ellen smirked. "Ah-ha! My babies *are* here."

She opened the door to the suite and tiptoed across the hardwood floor. Every now and then she paused and listened. She heard scratching coming from behind another door. She opened it, a huge smile on her face.

The room was jet black. There were no windows, and the faint light from the main part of the suite barely entered what appeared to be a storage room. She could barely make out the shelves that lined the wall closest to the door.

She reached for the light switch. *Darn. It's burnt out.*

Ellen stepped into the storage room. It was like being swallowed by a giant, complete with a faint but foul stench. This giant had bad breath.

Something rustled in the far corner.

"Molly?" she whispered. "Roxanne?"

Scratch, scratch...

Ellen tiptoed closer. "Mama's here."

She blinked to clear her vision, but the room was so dark she could only see a vague outline of a crate or box in the corner.

"Aw," she cooed. "Don't worry. I'll get you out."

Feeling her way, she reached the box, which rested horizontally on its side. Made of heavy cardboard, it was probably for a major appliance like a refrigerator.

The box trembled beneath her hand. "It's okay, babies. Mama's going to rescue you."

Fumbling in the dark, Ellen managed to pry open one flap, which had been taped. When she reached inside, she felt warm fur, and a small tongue licked her hand a bit too roughly. "Roxanne, is that you? Be nice."

She managed to open the second flap partway, but for some reason neither of her babies moved closer.

She released a huff. "Come on. I don't have all day."

Getting down on her knees, Ellen shuffled forward and stuck her head in the box. "Molly, Roxanne, come here. Come to Mama." She clapped her hands lightly.

Nothing.

"It's time to go home, babies."

She could hear them nibbling at something. They must have found a bone and brought it into the box. Or maybe this was where the Tremblays had kept them all along.

She leaned further inside, patting the cardboard floor as she went. A sticky residue coated her palms, but she ignored it and crawled slowly toward her pets.

Small eyes gleamed at her.

"Molly? Roxanne?"

Squinting, she noticed a lump a few feet away. She inched forward and nudged the lump. It rolled over, revealing the lifeless eyes of a bald-headed man. His mouth was open in a silent scream, and his face resembled raw ground beef. A pair of black-framed eyeglasses—one lens completely shattered—dangled off one ear. The man's head had been completely severed from his body.

An ear-piercing screech filled the room. *Hers!*

She muffled the sound with one hand and began scrabbling out of the box, her mind a whir of panic and wild thoughts. She knew one thing with absolute certainty. Those were not her babies inside that box. As she backed out of the box, hot waves of electric pain stabbed at her hands and arms.

Oh hell's bells!

Ellen was violently dragged deep inside the box.

Chapter 11
"Pain"

After a grueling hour at the dentist, Cathy climbed into the car and drove to the grocery store. Mike would be home tonight, and she wanted to make a special dinner. She picked up a couple of thick-cut T-bone steaks, two large baking potatoes already covered in foil, veggies for a salad and cheesecake for dessert.

When she returned home, she put the groceries away then poured a coffee and sat on the recliner. As her gaze swept across the room, she frowned. The energy seemed different somehow, as though the entire house tingled with a vibrancy she couldn't see.

It scared her.

Restless, she stood and paced around the living room, looking for a sign to explain her irrational fear. What was so different, so *wrong*?

She moved toward the stairs. With her head cocked, she listened.

Nothing.

She proceeded downstairs, pausing at the bottom to listen again.

There!

Soft noises came from deep within her mother's suite. Had her mother come home early?

A shiver ricocheted up Cathy's spine. *Or did someone break in?*

She opened the door as quietly as possible and stepped inside. Pale light peeked through the blinds, just enough for her to make out the furniture.

Thud!

The sound came from the storage room.

Inhaling deeply, she squared her shoulders and tiptoed across the room. A sliver of light shone beneath the storage room door. The light was interrupted by a moving shadow.

Shit! Someone's in there.

Grabbing the nearest heavy object, which happened to be her mother's Buddha sculpture, she raised it high over her head, ignored a hot stab of pain in her elbow and turned the doorknob with her fingertips.

She shoved the door open and charged forward.

No one was there.

The lights flickered on then off. That's what she'd seen beneath the door.

With a self-deprecating laugh, she left her mother's apartment and went upstairs. "Now I'm imagining things." She needed some fresh air.

Outside, the sun gleamed for a moment then disappeared behind a dense black cloud. A storm was coming. She wondered if it would reach West Kelowna or if it would stay on the Kelowna side.

The mailbox held no special treasures, only junk mail and two bills, so she strode down the street toward Ellen Wichman's home. Approaching the front door, she rang the doorbell. After a few seconds, no one answered, so she rang it a second time. Still no answer.

She walked around to the back, in case Ellen was busy in her garden.

"Ellen?"

No reply.

Maybe Ellen was picking up her poodles at the SPCA.

With a shrug, Cathy returned home.

Mike will be home in about an hour.

No sooner had this thought entered her mind than the phone rang.

"Please don't tell me you're going to be really late," she said. "I'm starving."

"I hope you didn't make any plans tonight," Mike replied.

"Not really. Why?"

"My truck's got a serious oil leak. I'll have to take a look at it tonight after supper, and I'll probably change the oil while I'm under there."

"Aw, I was hoping we could just chill tonight, relax."

"I'll relax once my truck's fixed. Speaking of relaxing, did you notice any house pests today?"

"No. I haven't even found a dead ant. And no signs of mice anywhere."

"Uh…Cathy? I should probably tell you…" His voice trailed away.

"Tell me what?"

"They weren't…mice. They were pack rats."

A hiss of air escaped between her teeth. "Rats? No way!"

"Yeah way. I found a female with babies in the garage. It wasn't until I spoke with your dad the other day that he confirmed my suspicions. He saw the one in the basement but didn't want to freak you out more than you already were."

"Ew!" Her eyes flitted around the room. "What did you do with the ones from the garage?"

"I, uh, disposed of them permanently."

"And there are no more rats in the house or garage?"

"Have you seen any?"

"No, thank God."

"Looks like we've finally got our house back to ourselves then."

"For one last night. Then Mom's home."

"Oh right. I forgot Margot was coming home tomorrow."

"So we'd better make the most of tonight."

"Now *that* sounds like a plan."

After they hung up, Cathy tossed the junk mail into the recycle bin and cranked up the radio. In the kitchen, she hummed along to the radio tunes while preparing the steaks and salad.

This was going to be a wonderful evening.

* * *

Mike arrived home at 6:30 p.m. His weary expression told Cathy he needed nothing more than to fill his belly and relax, but she could tell by his restlessness that he had other plans.

"Dinner's ready," she said.

"Great."

She handed him a loaded plate. "Want to watch *Castle* while we eat?"

"Maybe once I'm done with my truck," he said between mouthfuls.

"So you're going to wolf down this awesome meal I made then leave me?"

He shot her an apologetic smile. "Hopefully it'll be an easy fix."

"Ha! I know what happens when you go out to the garage." She snorted. "You'll find a million other things wrong with your truck, and you'll decide to fix them all. Tonight."

"Needs to be done. I can't ignore the way it's driving."

"Are you sure I can't persuade you some *other* way?" She arched her brow suggestively.

"You can try," Mike said, grinning.

After supper, Cathy sat on a barstool by the island and refilled her vaporizer. She stretched out a hand to shake off the placemat. *Snap!* A subtle shift of the wooden stool indicated something had broken. From that point on, everything happened in slow motion. At least that's how it felt.

She began to slide to the left. She reached out, instinctively clawing at the countertop and hooking her feet around the stool legs. Bad move. One of the legs gave way, and ever so slowly she began to fall…down…down…to the floor.

When she hit the hardwood surface, she felt her body *slide* more than *thud*, but as she fell, her hands swept everything off the counter and onto the floor. The clatter of small items and shattered glass was more deafening than anything else.

Mike ran into the kitchen and found her on the floor. "Are you all right?"

Cathy's left arm propped up her head. Her legs were stretched out behind her, while she tried hard not to laugh. "I'm fine. But I think I broke the stool."

He reached out a hand, but she waved it away. "I just want to lie here a minute before I try to move."

The view from the floor wasn't very appealing, but she didn't want to rush things, in case she'd hurt more than her dignity. When she finally moved, she felt a twinge in her right ankle and ribs. Nothing was broken—just sore.

"I'm surprised you didn't do a chalk outline while I was down there," she joked.

He gave her a worried look. "You sure you're okay?"

"Yeah. Damned stool."

Embarrassment washed over her when she caught sight of the broken stool.

Mike picked up the wooden leg and turned it over. "This was bound to break eventually."

Cathy arched a brow. "You saying I need to go on a diet?"

"No. I'm saying the previous owners' dogs must have been chewing on this." He showed her the chair leg where small tooth marks had gouged out a chunk of wood.

"That's not from a dog," she said, her voice grave. "I washed both stools when we moved in and there wasn't a mark on them. And we don't have a dog."

"But we do have—"

"Rats," she finished. "And carpenter ants. It's almost like they did it on purpose, so I'd fall."

"That's just too weird."

Mike picked up broken stool parts and its companion. "I'm throwing them both out. We don't need this to happen again."

"Okay." She hobbled over to the reclining sofa, sat down and raised her feet. "This is where I'll be until bedtime."

"Well, if you're okay then I'm heading out to the garage."

"I'm fine. But if you find my dignity anywhere, let me know."

* * *

From the main tunnel, it called to the other residents of the house on Horizon Drive. Tonight they hid in the shadowed recesses of the tunnel maze, waiting for the sun to set. They always came out when rooms were pitch black or during the night when the moon was high. Creatures of the shadows, many had newborns, and most were in pain, starving…ravenous.

They were carnivorous creatures that scavenged for scraps of food, and newly slaughtered meat was their favorite. They didn't care what kind. Hunger drove them to seek out any form of protein.

It promised them a bountiful banquet of one of their favorite meats.

Their tiny mouths salivated almost painfully. *Fresh, raw, warm meat.*

Tonight, they would feast.

Chapter 12
"S.O.B."

Mike turned on the grime-covered radio above his workbench, and the garage was instantly filled with a mix of classic and new rock. He wasn't into that pop fluff that Cathy seemed to enjoy.

He retrieved an unopened bottle of motor oil from the top shelf over the workbench. A wrench hung on a hook below the shelf. Next, he located the drip pan and spare filter. These were still in a box he hadn't yet unpacked. He placed everything on the concrete floor beside the truck.

Okay, what else?

He pulled a pair of navy-blue coveralls over his clothes and stuffed a rag in a front pocket, along with a spare gasket. Then he grabbed the jack from the back of the truck and positioned it in front of the vehicle. He cranked it, raising the truck about a foot off the ground. After locking the jack in place, he leaned on the hood and applied pressure to confirm the jack would hold. It did.

Opening the hood, he removed the oil cap. Finally, he positioned a flashlight so it shone underneath the truck. "Let there be light."

All he needed now were a couple of safety blocks.

Mike spent the next fifteen minutes going through the boxes in the garage, but he came up empty. No blocks.

Well, crap. This has to be done tonight.

He assessed the situation. The jack was locked and his bounce test proved the truck wouldn't go anywhere. Besides, he'd performed this task a hundred times, along with regular maintenance on their vehicles, and he wouldn't be under the vehicle for very long.

Repairing his twenty-year-old Ford often took some ingenuity, and Mike had that in spades. Cathy often referred to him as

"Mike-gyver" when he was working on vehicles. Sometimes all one needed was a pair of pantyhose and a stick of chewing gum—or duct tape.

As for changing the oil? Piece of cake. He knew the mantra inside out.

Remove drain plug with wrench, drain oil into pan, wipe with rag, replace plug, remove old filter and replace, then add fresh oil.

A padded chrome creeper hung from a rusty nail on the wall to the left of the workbench. He tested the wheels to ensure a smooth ride then rolled the creeper beside the truck. Lowering himself onto it, he groaned, stretched out on his back and slid beneath the vehicle.

The source of the oil leak became crystal clear the second he swiped at a glob of grease on the oil pan. "The drain plug's loose."

Finally, luck was on *his* side. This was an easy fix.

It was while he was removing the plug that he felt the ground begin to vibrate, the wheels of the creeper tapping against the concrete.

Earthquake? He snickered at the absurdity. *Nah, it's only traffic.*

Without warning, the garage lights flickered.

Mike paused, thankful for the flashlight. *Power failure?*

He cranked his head to one side and peered up at the radio. Though the ceiling lights still flickered, the digital display on the radio remained stable. So either there was a storm outside or there was a short somewhere in the wiring.

The drip pan shifted suddenly, and oil splattered his coveralls. *Shit!*

With a groan of frustration, he reached for the rag again. "Ow!" He snatched his hand back, noting the blood streaming down the side of his hand. What the hell had he caught it on?

He lifted his head a few inches, but in the dim light he couldn't see past his stomach. Whatever he'd sliced his hand on was probably on the floor by now. He'd sweep it up later.

With careful movements, he removed the rag from the pocket and examined it. There were no wood splinters or metal shards on the cloth. He wiped the blood from his hand and set the rag on his chest.

The radio let out a harsh squawk, followed by distortion.

Beneath the truck, Mike cringed. As soon as he was done, he'd turn the irritating thing off.

The garage lights flickered again then went out.

As long as the flashlight doesn't die, I'm good.

He was almost finished anyway.

Once the oil stopped dripping into the pan, he mopped up any greasy residue on the parts. He slid the pan out from underneath the truck. The gasket needed replacing so he retrieved the spare from another pocket. Cleaning the metal washer, he replaced it and tightened the plug.

Next, the filter.

A soft thud came from the far corner, but he shrugged it off.

He began unscrewing the oil filter.

The static on the radio cleared. He recognized the song playing, but it took a minute for the title and artist's name to come to him. "S.O.B." by Nathaniel Rateliff and The Night Sweats. As he listened, he had to give the artist credit. Rateliff had the perfect voice for such a song.

"Son of a bitch, give me a drink…"

A slight breeze brushed his face as something skittered past his head. When he cocked his head for a better view, he saw a trembling black mass slithering toward him. *What the hell is that?*

He tried to push the creeper from underneath the vehicle, but it wouldn't budge. Straining, he pushed and pulled, desperate to escape the looming shadow. He reached out and knocked the flashlight over, its beam landing on the mass and finally revealing his attackers.

Rats.

Dozens of the rodents surrounded him on all sides. Their stench was overpowering, and Mike gagged. One fat rat crawled next to his face. It stared at him for a long moment.

"Get away! Get off me"

The rat tipped its head to one side, its black eyes unwavering.

"What the fuck do you want?" Mike yelled.

Twisting his head to one side, he watched more rats encompass the jack, and he heard the unmistakable sound of it unlocking.

Fear flooded his mind, followed by resignation. *Son of a bitch.*

The truck crashed down on him, crushing his legs, arms, stomach and chest. He'd managed to turn his head in time, and when he found his breath, a horrifying shriek escaped his lips. "Cathy! Help me!"

Minuscule feet tickled his arms and legs, and even in his state of shock, Mike knew they were ants. Spiders came next, pooling around his head. They climbed into his ears and meandered up his nose. He coughed and gagged as rodents and insects feasted on his body.

Welcome to the all-you-can-eat Mike Tremblay buffet. He tried to emit a half-crazed laugh, but his mouth was stuffed with foreign bodies.

A large, fat rat approached. It sat on shaggy haunches a few inches from his face, staring at Mike with an intensity that suggested intelligence.

Mike nodded in recognition. *I know. I killed your family. I'm sorry.*

The rat's nose twitched. Then it lunged for his throat.

Frenzied ants and spiders joined in.

As Mike lay dying, a raspy male voice sang, *"My heart was breaking, hands are shaking, bugs are crawling all over me..."*

Chapter 13
"The House of the Rising Sun"

At midnight, Cathy pressed an ear to the garage door. She heard the radio first and then Mike puttering around. He was still working on the truck.

Damn...

She'd already managed to watch three recorded shows before deciding she'd had enough. She was bone tired and ready for sleep in her now pest-free home, and she wanted nothing more than to curl up with Mike. She always slept better when he was home.

She turned out all but one light in the living room and felt her way to the bedroom, where she slipped into a black-satin negligee and climbed between the sheets. With light only from her Kindle Fire, she opened the first page of *Avalanche*, a new thriller by Kristina Stanley. Confident that Stanley's fast pace and the icy mountain setting of Stone Mountain Resort would keep her awake, she read and waited for Mike.

Forty minutes later, she yawned. The words on the Kindle were beginning to blur.

When the heck is Mike coming to bed?

Her husband's natural talent as a mechanic had come in handy over the years, but she was always nervous about going to sleep when he was in the garage. He always lost track of time out there. And what if he hurt himself?

Yeah, no way I'm sleeping.

She set the Kindle on the nightstand, turned on the TV and knocked off an episode of *NCIS*. By this time, she was so tired she could barely keep her eyes open. She'd even missed bits and pieces of the show.

"Come on, Mike," she murmured, switching the TV to a music station.

With reckless abandon, she strode out of the bedroom with one thing on her mind. Okay, two. First, she hoped to God none of her neighbors in the valley had telescopes or binoculars trained on her windows, because the negligee was extremely revealing. Second, she'd make Mike forget all about that bothersome truck.

Groping her way down the hallway, she reached the living room that was still lit by the table lamp. As she passed the foyer, an odd sight made her pause. Her father's laptop case sat on the bench by the front door. When she moved it, she realized the laptop was inside.

What the hell?

Her father *never* left his laptop behind. It was his most precious possession.

"Double-Oh-Zero must have Old Timer's," she muttered. *I'll call him in the morning.*

She continued toward the door to the garage. Music emanated from behind the door, and she recognized the song that was playing. *House of the Rising Sun* by Five Finger Death Punch. It was one of her favorites.

She opened the door. "Mike? Are you almost finished?"

The garage lights flickered erratically in response, casting shadows all around the garage.

"Did you hear me?"

Mike's legs protruded from under his work truck, but he didn't move.

She frowned. "Hey! I'm getting really cold. Come to bed."

No reply.

Cathy swallowed hard. Something was very wrong.

Grabbing her jacket from the hook on the wall near the door, she wrapped it around her shoulders and took a step into the garage. It took a minute to register that her worst nightmare had come true.

Her husband's legs weren't moving because the truck was crushing him.

"Mike!" she yelled.

Crouching low, she locked eyes with Mike, whose vacant gaze told her he was in shock. Blood seeped from his mouth, while an occasional hiss of air escaped his lips.

"Oh God! Hold on, Mike. I'm calling 911."

As she straightened, movement in the corner by the irrigation panel made her hesitate. *What the heck...?*

A wave of ravenous death came for her in one fluid motion.

Cathy cried out when the shadow broke into many smaller shapes, which soon became distinct in the beam from the flashlight.

Rats, spiders...ants.

She ran into the house and locked the door to the garage.

"This is *our* house," she muttered between gritted teeth. "Not yours."

The hall light flickered once then died. The power was out.

"Shit!" Where the hell had she left her cell phone?

In the living room, she checked the counters and charger. No phone.

Her pulse pounded. Mike was hurt—maybe dying—and she couldn't find her goddamn phone. *Bedroom!*

As she moved out of the kitchen, she felt a draft of humid, dank-smelling air. Then she heard scratching coming behind the kitchen cabinets. Fuck! She'd forgotten about the crack in the wall of the small closet. From underneath the pantry door, ants and spiders scrambled out and made a beeline for her.

She turned and headed for her bedroom. Crossing the living room, she heard thumping sounds coming from behind the couch. *The vents!* The instant the thought entered her mind, dozens of rats crawled out of the floor vents.

With a wail of panic, she sprinted down the hallway to the bedroom. Slamming the door behind her, she locked it. Her heart was beating so quickly she was afraid she'd pass out. She snatched her robe from the hook on the door and stuffed her arms into, tightening the belt around her waist. Then she grabbed Mike's robe and stuffed it underneath the door.

She spotted her cell phone on the nightstand. Above it, small white spiders poured out of her sleep apnea mask. *Oh my God...*

As she reached for the phone, her bare feet and legs were attacked. She batted at the carpenter ants feeding on her skin and accidentally knocked her phone on the floor. It skittered under the bed.

Aw, shit.

Dropping to her knees, Cathy squished as many ants and spiders as she could, then stretched out an arm, the cell phone just inches from her fingertips. The two floor vents by the window vomited up an army of ants, and they were headed straight for her.

Come on! Get the phone!

As the voracious hoard undulated closer with unbelievable speed, she cried out, "Mike!"

A weight landed on her back, and she let out another yelp. This was followed by a shrill scream that echoed through the room as sharp teeth bit into her buttocks and back. She could feel their dirty fur rubbing against her naked skin. The rats were joined by thousands of ants and spiders that crawled into her ears and up her nose. She choked and gagged, scraping her nails against the flesh of her ears and face. Her hand came away covered in blood.

She recalled the strange disappearance of the previous owners. They'd vanished without a trace. What had happened to them?

Her mind numb with agonizing pain, she realized something else. She'd been right that the house was infested. But now she knew who the real threat was.

Mike and me, we're the house pests. We invaded their home. We're the true infestation.

She couldn't feel the animals eating her anymore. Instead, she felt peace wash over her, and in the distance she could hear music. The music channel on the TV was playing "Infestation," sung by a guy with a low, eerie voice. It was new, and she'd gotten a kick out of the lyrics because of how it applied to their unwanted house pest guests, even though the song was about an evil, *Basic-Instinct*-style seductress.

It wasn't so humorous now. The lyrics filled her with dread.

"Your scent it swarms me in a vile embrace. You are an outbreak with an evil face..."

Rats, ants and spiders swarmed her body until she was completely covered.

She took in a ragged breath of air and croaked, "I love you, Mike."

Her ears bursting with ants, she exhaled one last time as the song came to an end.

"You are the Reaper, and your name is Death."

Epilogue
"The Sound of Silence"

The following morning, while most residents of West Kelowna still slept, early risers ignored the looming darkness and prepared to head off to work—including Les, the Tremblays' neighbor. As Les backed his truck out of the garage, something caught his eye. He stomped on the brakes and gaped at his neighbors' yard.

"No way," he whispered.

Parking on the driveway, Les climbed out of the truck, his legs and hands shaking with fear. He took a few wobbly steps toward the Tremblay property, his mouth gaping in horror. "Oh my God…"

The Tremblays' 3200-square-foot house with walkout basement was now a murky mound of damp dirt. To an unsuspecting eye, the lot looked as though it had never been occupied. The entire yard was leveled, except for the mound where the house had once stood.

A car horn blared, and Les jumped. A canary-yellow taxi pull up to the curb. He muttered a curse when he recognized the occupant. Sixty-four-year-old Margot Kilborn, Cathy's mother, stepped out of the taxi, her jaw slack with astonishment.

"Les! What happened?" she cried out. "Where the heck is the house? And Cathy and Mike?"

"I have no idea. The house was here when I went to bed last night."

Margot frowned. "They never said anything to me about demolishing it while I was gone."

"Me neither."

"I know they wanted to build a new home one day, but I didn't expect them to do it when I was on holiday." She gave him a mournful look. "I really loved my apartment here."

Les opened his mouth to say something then closed it. What could he say? He didn't know what the hell was going on.

"I'm going to find Cathy and Mike," Margot said, determination gleaming in her eyes, "and give them a piece of my mind. They're probably staying with their friends, Dina and Bo, during the renovations. They'll be lucky if I don't decide to move out on my own." With an irritated sigh, she climbed back into the taxi, and the vehicle sped off.

Les had a strong feeling that Margot was the lucky one. Whatever had happened to the Tremblay home, it wasn't natural. Something was very, very wrong with the whole scenario.

He returned his gaze to the lot next door. He willed his legs to move closer so he could inspect the mound. That's when he noticed the earth was writhing and churning, and the air was thick with the stench of fresh soil and decay.

Earthquake?

With a frown etching his face, he took another step forward. The wriggling ground vomited up twisting tendrils that lunged for his feet. But it wasn't dirt. Millions of ants, spiders, maggots, flies and rats erupted from the earth. With lightning speed, they sucked at his shoes and dragged him down onto his back.

In the blink of an eye, they scrabbled up his legs and onto his chest, their weight crushing his ribs. They bit and chewed his clothing and then his flesh. They trailed across his face, into his ears, up his nose. They made faint clicking sounds as they feasted.

"Get off me!" he shrieked, clawing at his face. His fingernails left trails of blood that only incited them even more.

As the sun finally rose, Les's hoarse cries echoed through the peaceful Okanagan Valley, followed by the sound of silence.

~ * ~

If you enjoyed this book, please consider writing a short review and posting it on your favorite review site. Reviews are very helpful to other readers and are greatly appreciated by authors, especially me. When you post a review, drop me an email and let me know and I may feature part of it on my blog/site. Thank you.

cherylktardif@shaw.ca

Message from the Author

Dear Reader,

I hope you enjoyed this story, which was inspired by *true* events. But, of course, it's not ALL true. ☺ I'll leave you to determine what is fiction and what is fact.

INFESTATION describes events that occurred after my husband, Marc, and I bought a pre-owned home in West Kelowna in 2015. However, some elements have been fictionalized, and some names have been changed to protect the innocent—and not so innocent.

After enduring **five** separate episodes of the various pests mentioned in this novella, I was motivated to turn the unpleasant experience into something positive. So I returned to my writing roots as a horror author, inspired by Stephen King, Dean Koontz and John Grisham, who have given me decades of goosebumps, thrills and chills—not to mention, plenty of nightmares.

Why do we do this to ourselves? Why do we read horror novels or watch horror movies? Maybe we expose ourselves to dread and fear so we can overcome these emotions. Perhaps our brains are hardwired to experience horror in a way that seems almost…pleasurable. It's also feasible that we need these terror-filled books and movies so our daily lives don't seem to be mundane and ordinary.

Whatever the reason, I have loved being scared by these masters of horror.

With this work, I endeavored to terrify you. I wanted you to *feel* what I felt, and what my *characters* felt—every hair-raising, spine-tingling, creepy, crawly sensation. If reading this novella made you scratch and itch, then I have succeeded. Oh, and I also wanted you to laugh out loud at times. Did you? ☺

Drop me an email at cherylktardif@shaw.ca, or connect with me at https://www.facebook.com/cherylkayetardif (Facebook) or http://www.twitter.com/cherylktardif (Twitter). I love hearing from readers.

Happy reading!

~ Cheryl Kaye Tardif

PS: In case you missed it, every chapter in *INFESTATION* is named after a popular song. For the complete soundtrack list with links to YouTube, turn the page.

Chapter Soundtrack

Prologue – "Secrets" by OneRepublic
Chapter 1 – "Mama, I'm Comin' Home" by Ozzie Osbourne
Chapter 2 – "Trouble" by Coldplay
Chapter 3 – "2 Heads" by Coleman Hell
Chapter 4 – "Fly Away" by Lenny Kravitz
Chapter 5 – "Radioactive" by Imagine Dragons
Chapter 6 – "Wings of a Butterfly" by HIM
Chapter 7 – "Walk Away" by Christina Aguilera
Chapter 8 – "I Will Not Bow" by Breaking Benjamin
Chapter 9 – "Crawling" by Linkin Park
Chapter 10 – "Electric Love" by BØRNS
Chapter 11 – "Pain" by Three Days Grace
Chapter 12 – "S.O.B." by Nathaniel Rateliff and The Night Sweats
Chapter 13 – "House of the Rising Sun" by Five Finger Death Punch (fast-forward through the intro part—*strong language*)
Epilogue – "The Sound of Silence" by Disturbed

Works by Cheryl Kaye Tardif

Novels:
SUBMERGED
CHILDREN OF THE FOG
WHALE SONG (Includes WHALE SONG: School Edition [with discussion guide for schools and book clubs] and Large Print edition)
DIVINE INTERVENTION
DIVINE JUSTICE
DIVINE SANCTUARY
THE RIVER
LANCELOT'S LADY

Anthologies or Collections:
SKELETONS IN THE CLOSET & OTHER CREEPY STORIES
WHAT FEARS BECOME
SHADOW MASTERS
A FEAST OF FRIGHTS FROM THE HORROR ZINE
25 YEARS IN THE REARVIEW MIRROR: 52 Authors Look Back

Bundles & Trilogies:
DIVINE TRILOGY
DEADLY DOZEN: 12 Mystery/Thriller Novels
SWEET & SENSUAL: 6 Romance Novels

Qwickie® Novellas:
INFESTATION
EAGLE E.Y.E
E.Y.E. OF THE SCORPION

Short Stories:
DREAM HOUSE
REMOTE CONTROL

Children's Books:
THE ELFLING PRINCESS

Foreign Translations:
VERSUNKEN (German – Submerged)
LES ENFANTS DU BROUILLARD (French - Children of the Fog)
DIVINE: Blick ins Feuer (German - Divine Intervention)
WILDER FLUSS (German - The River)
DES NEBELS KINDER (German - Children of the Fog)
DIE MELODIE DER WALE (German - Whale Song)
DIE MELODIE DER WALE: Schulausgabe (German - Whale Song: School Edition)
LANCELOTS LADY (German - Lancelot's Lady)
GIZEMLI NEHIR (Turkish - The River)

Non-Fiction:
HOW I MADE OVER $42,000 IN 1 MONTH SELLING MY KINDLE eBOOKS

Audio Books:
CHILDREN OF THE FOG
SUBMERGED
DES NEBELS KINDER (German – Children of the Fog)

About the Author

Cheryl Kaye Tardif is an award-winning, international bestselling Canadian suspense author published by various publishers. Some of her most popular novels have been translated into foreign languages. She is best known for CHILDREN OF THE FOG (over 150,000 copies sold worldwide) and WHALE SONG.

When people ask her what she does, Cheryl likes to say, "I kill people off for a living!" You can imagine the looks she gets. Sometimes she'll add, "Fictitiously, of course. I'm a suspense author." Sometimes she won't say anything else.

Inspired by Stephen King, Dean Koontz and others, Cheryl strives to create stories that feel real, characters you'll love or hate, and a pace that will keep you reading.

In 2014, she penned her first "Qwickie" (novella) for Imajin Books™ new imprint, Imajin Qwickies™. *E.Y.E. of the Scorpion* is the first in her E.Y.E. Spy Mystery series.

Cheryl recently moved back to her home province of BC, where she enjoys her new home in West Kelowna. She's now working on her next thriller.

Booklist raves, "Tardif, already a big hit in Canada…a name to reckon with south of the border."

Cheryl's website: www.cherylktardif.com
Blog: www.cherylktardif.blogspot.com
Twitter: www.twitter.com/cherylktardif
Facebook:
https://www.facebook.com/CherylKayeTardif

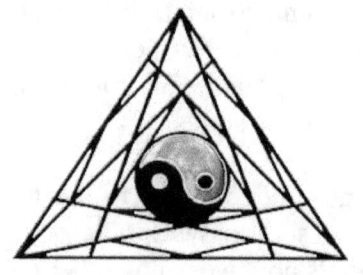

IMAJIN BOOKS®

Quality fiction beyond your wildest dreams

For your next eBook or paperback purchase, please visit:

www.imajinbooks.com

www.imajinbooks.blogspot.com

www.twitter.com/imajinbooks

www.facebook.com/imajinbooks

IMAJIN QWICKIES®
www.ImajinQwickies.com